Twinkle, Twinkle, Little Star
# There's a Body
# in the Car

Twinkle, Twinkle, Little Star
# There's a Body in the Car

A Callie Parrish Mystery

# *Fran Rizer*

BellaRosaBooks

BellaRosaBooks

Twinkle, Twinkle, Little Star There's A Body In The Car
ISBN 978-1-933523-94-1

First printed January 2011

Library of Congress Control Number: 2010942076

Printed in the United States of America on acid-free paper.

Cover illustrations by Joyce Wright – www.artbyjoyce.com

BellaRosaBooks and logo are trademarks of Bella Rosa Books.

10      9      8      7      6      5      4      3      2      1

Dedicated to the Memory of

Linda C. Derrick

1946 - 2009

Twinkle, Twinkle, Little Star
# There's a Body
# in the Car

# Chapter One

A fly sat on the old geezer's nose. I saw it the minute I hopped out of my vintage Mustang and glanced over at the silver-blue Jag, an XF, parked beside me in front of Best Bargain Books. I was headed there to buy a couple of used mysteries to keep my mind off all my worries—like did I need to go to Atlanta to talk to my favorite brother John about his marital problems? Should I change my bra and panties? *Did I actually say that? Ex-cuuse me. I wear fresh ones every day. I meant should I change the style of my underwear back to inflatable bras and panties with fanny padding. I'm straight and flat, going or coming, but I quit wearing augmented garments a while back.*

The man took my thoughts off myself, including whether Molly *really* planned to have a poodle as one of the bridal attendants at the wedding and would *I* have to stand by the dog.

I don't know why I thought of the man as an old geezer. He could just as easily be called an elderly gentleman, who had probably driven that high-dollar executive car from Hilton Head, where people richer than us live. The gray-haired man sat in his Jaguar with the windows up and the air conditioning running to protect him from the unseasonably sweltering heat of the South Carolina coast. October felt like July during this heat wave. Perhaps his wife was shopping around in the strip mall before they headed back to more luxurious beach areas than St. Mary offers.

Sometimes my mind flits around like a gnat. I remembered studying flies in school and reading that when they land on something, they regurgitate. As a little girl, that fact had made me sit by the picnic table with a fly-swatter—which I used to call a fly-flapper—while my five older brothers ran around having fun.

Now I wondered why the man didn't swat that fly off his nose. It was crawling around on his big ole honker, no doubt heaving insect throw-up as it moved. The man's eyes were closed, so he may have been asleep, but I'd bet an insect on my nose would have awakened me.

"Hey, you," I called as I stepped up to the driver's side of the car. He didn't move. I dropped my purse to the ground, grasped the door handle with both hands and yanked, but it was locked. I rapped on the window glass, then tried to shake the car by bumping my hip up against the door. The man slumped forward, and his chest and head landed on the steering wheel. The horn blared, and the fly flew off his nose. I didn't know whether that was because of the sound or the man's movement, but his eyes stayed closed.

Best, the muscle-bound bookstore owner, opened the front door of his shop and stuck his head out. "What's all that noise?" he yelled, then recognized me. "Oh, it's you, Callie Parrish. Are you trying to steal that car?"

Like I'd ever do that! Now, Jane, my BFF (best friend forever), is a different story, but since she's totally, completely blind, the last thing she'd need to pilfer was a vehicle, even a luxurious one like that Jaguar. Besides, to give the devil his, or should I say *her* due, though I'd tried and tried unsuccessfully to make Jane quit shoplifting, I'd never known her to filch anything big or expensive.

"I *said* what are you doing with that car?" Best yelled.

That wasn't exactly what he'd said, but I'm not arguing with the Hulk—the green one or the blond one. I answered, "I think this man is sick or passed out or something."

Best stepped to the car quickly. As usual, he was wearing fitted jeans and a black T-shirt molded to every defined bicep and ab. He held a hardback book in his right hand. Looking through the driver's window, he said, "Go use the phone in the store. Call 911 for an ambulance." Then Best slammed the book into the window, setting off the car alarm and showering the inside of the car with chunks of glass. The older man still didn't move. Just sat there with pieces of glass shimmering like diamonds against his brown and tan plaid walking shorts and forest green Hilton Head Dunes golf shirt.

I confess. I've never been really good about following directions, especially not immediately. I work for Middleton's Mortuary as a cosmetition, which is Funeralese for cosmetologist, so I've seen lots of deceased people. This man looked more dead than asleep or sick. I knocked the remaining shattered glass out of the window, trying to direct the pieces down close to the door so they wouldn't land on him. When I reached through the broken window and touched the old man's cheek, the skin was hard. Rigor mortis.

"Okay," I said as Best crowded beside me and reached through the window, opened the door, and leaned over the body. "I'll call 911, but we need the coroner, not an ambulance."

Best jumped back and almost knocked me over. He shoved me behind him. *Good grief!* I thought. *This man's built like Hulk Hogan, and he's scared of a corpse.*

I stepped around him to get back to the car, but he yanked me away.

"Don't open the door, Callie. There's a snake in

there."

Shrugging away from Best's grip, I looked through the window. I didn't see a snake, just a dead man.

"Probably a corn snake or something," I mumbled as I reached for the handle of the door.

"Red and yellow, kill a fellow," Best said and pulled me even farther from the Jag.

Every kid who grew up on the South Carolina coast knew at least one of those rhymes. We learned them in school to distinguish the venomous Eastern Coral Snakes from their imitators, the Scarlet Snakes and the Scarlet King Snakes. All three species are striped bright red, yellow, and black. Yellow-red-yellow identifies the poisonous Eastern Coral while the two harmless snakes have black bordering the red, as in black-red-black. Rhymes about the order of the stripes were the standard way most people distinguished poisonous from harmless.

"I don't see any snake, but the man's dead anyway," I said. "I'll call the sheriff's office." I was dressed for work—black dress with low black heels—and I didn't have any pockets. I picked my purse up from the pavement and rummaged for the cell phone. I'd forgotten it again.

Stepping into the building, I called out, "Hey, is anybody with the older man in the Jaguar out front?" No one answered. I didn't see anyone, but with all the book racks, it's impossible to view the entire store. I grabbed the phone beside the cash register, dialed 911, and reported the body.

As I hung up, Best came in. "Don't you think someone should be out there with the man?" I asked.

"Go on back then. You said he's dead and you should know. I'll stay in here where it's cool."

"I thought he might be waiting for someone in the store," I commented.

"Nobody in here. You're today's first customer, and that car was there when I got here to open up. Couldn't help but notice wheels like that."

"What time was it?"

"Not more than ten minutes before you started making all that commotion. What are you doing, Callie? Playing detective again?"

I didn't have to answer that sassy comment because a siren and screeching tires announced the arrival of Jade County's finest. I followed Best back out to the parking lot. A squad car slammed on brakes behind the Jag. A slim, uniformed deputy jumped out and rushed to the body. He'd reached for the door handle when Best said, "There's a coral snake in the car."

"They're poisonous, aren't they?" the man asked with a pronounced Yankee accent. I nodded.

The officer's face showed more age than his youthful energy indicated. I'd never seen him before, and frequently new deputies are younger than this man's probable forty years or so. "Blake" was printed on his name tag.

"Yes," I answered, "but they aren't very aggressive. Probably won't bite you unless you bother it."

The sun was scorching. The deputy wiped sweat off his forehead and said something, but I couldn't hear him over the sound of more sirens as Sheriff Harmon, a fire truck, and an EMS vehicle all pulled up. Two paramedics hit the pavement, both carrying medical equipment bags, and ran toward the Jaguar. Their rush ended when they reached the elderly man. One of them looked over at the sheriff, frowned, and shook his head no.

"I coulda told you that," I said. "Rigor's set in. Rigor mortis stiffening of muscles starts at the top of the body with the eyelids, neck and jaw before it moves down. His face is already stiff, but his arm isn't. It generally takes several hours for full rigor to set in and another twenty-four to eighty-four hours for the muscles to relax and become flaccid. The process can be hastened or slowed by conditions at death." I paused for breath.

"Thank you, Miss Callie, for that informative lesson," Sheriff Harmon said sarcastically. "I guess I already know about rigor mortis, what with being an officer of the law and all." He stopped and stared at me for a minute or so. "Did you dye your hair again?" he asked.

"No," I said, "I never 'dye' my hair. I've tinted it back to auburn because I got tired of the blonde." Being a cosmetologist, I change my hair color frequently.

The sheriff and I are old friends. He used to hang around with my older brothers when I was growing up. He called me Miss Callie as a reference to my having been a kindergarten teacher before I started working at the mortuary. "What are you doing here?" he added.

I gestured toward the bookstore and answered, "I came to buy something to read."

"And you found a body?" His tone wasn't exactly mocking this time, but it wasn't professional either.

"Sure did. I saw the man when I pulled in and wondered if he was sleeping. Then I thought he might be sick. Best broke the window so we could check him, but the old gentleman's dead."

"Somehow I'm not surprised," the sheriff said. "Sit down in your car or go wait in the store. I've got to call the coroner, but I'll need a statement from you before you leave."

In the bookstore, I checked over the used mysteries, looking for something I didn't already have. Concentration was difficult with my eyes constantly drawn to the window to see what was going on outside. I abandoned the discount shelves and grabbed a new Janet Evanovich. When Best and the deputy came in, they sat down in one of the reading centers. I moved behind a book rack near them so I could dip into their conversation.

"Your name, Sir?"

"Best. Finelay Best."

"Could you spell that, Sir?"

"You say it like Finn—lee, but it's spelled F-I-N-E-L-A-Y. Like fine lay." Best laughed. He always did when he said this, which was often. "On the rolls in high school, my name was Best Fine Lay, and the young ladies could tell you I was well-named."

The deputy ignored Best's silly bragging, which was the reason I always called him "Best." I must have heard about Best Fine Lay a million times. Well, maybe not a million, but at least a few thousand.

I'm as curious as a cat and—buh-leeve me—I've probably used up most of my nine lives already. I planned to eavesdrop on Best's statement even though I couldn't think of anything he'd lie about. The sheriff squelched my plans by coming in and calling, "Callie? Callie, come here."

"Yes?" I answered and stepped out from behind the book rack.

"The coroner's on the way, and I've called Middleton's to pick up the corpse." Nothing surprising in that. Otis and Odell, my bosses at Middleton's Mortuary, had won the county bid on transporting bodies from St. Mary to MUSC, the Medical University of South Carolina, in Charleston, when a postmortem was required. An autopsy is *always* required when the cause of death isn't blatant and obvious.

"Un-huh?" I muttered, trying to encourage Harmon to tell me what that had to do with me.

"Otis has the flu, and Odell's already sent Jake to pick up a body from the hospital in Beaufort. Odell's by himself and needs you to come straight to work so he can bring the other hearse over here." He paused. "I'll come by the funeral home later to take your statement."

*Dalmation!* I thought in kindergarten cussing. I wanted to hang around and play investigator, but I said, "You got it!" and hurried out to my Mustang.

Turning into the parking lot, I was impressed as always by the beauty of the mortuary. A huge, white two-story building with columns and a wrap-around veranda, it typified the Old South. White rocking chairs on the porch reminded me of the Cracker Barrel, and the huge planters overflowing with seasonal annuals, bronze and yellow mums for October, added color. Gigantic live oak trees draped in Spanish moss surrounded the lot.

As I entered the building, I met Odell coming out the back door. "Take care of things, Callie," he said. He was half-way down the steps when he turned around and added, "I sent Jake to pick up a Mr. Joyner from the hospital. Mrs. Joyner called. The fool woman wants a St. Patrick's Day funeral for her husband. Makes no sense to me. I told her to call back in about an hour to set up an appointment for planning. Otis has the stomach-flu. I don't think he'll be in, but if he comes, tell him to leave the fellow in the cooler. The wife doesn't want him embalmed."

"Maybe she's Irish," I suggested. "Do they embalm in Ireland?"

"Or maybe she's crazy," Odell growled, ignoring my question, as he got into the funeral coach (proper Funeralese for hearse). I headed toward my office to await the call from a lady who wanted a St. Patrick's Day funeral in October.

# Chapter Two

*Brrrrr!*

Odell is forty to fifty pounds overweight, and he sets the air conditioning on "frigid" when Otis isn't there. We keep the air conditioning turned up—or is it turned down?—in the funeral home. I never know how to say it. Does turning the air up mean that the thermostat is set at a higher number, therefore making it warmer? Or does it mean turning the unit up to work harder creating colder air?

In any event, Odell wants the place to feel like a deep freezer. I'd barely stepped through the back employee entrance before I scurried to the thermostat to adjust it before my nippies froze and fell off. Then I went to my office and pulled a black sweater over my dress until I warmed up.

I'd just put my books and purse in the bottom drawer of my desk when a soft, instrumental version of "My Soul Will Fly Free" sounded. Recorded hymns and gospel songs play throughout the building when the front door is opened. The system was in place when I came to work a few years earlier, and I much preferred the music to having a doorbell or chimes announce a visitor.

The Middleton twins, Otis and Odell, have made some improvements and modernized the services with changes like online obituaries and condolence registers since I came to work. They recently bought a large plasma screen television for Slumber Room A to show video memorials, but the furnishings remain basically the same as when their parents ran the mortuary. The dark woods and mahogany of beautifully upholstered antique chairs and tables shine impeccably thanks to the daily polishing by our part-time cleaning woman.

A lady sat beside the hall tree. The stuffed chair overwhelmed her petite size. She looked up at me from under thick, full gray bangs that covered her forehead and touched her eyebrows. She appeared to be in her late fifties.

"May I help you?" I asked.

"I hope so," she said as she stood and offered me her hand for a strong handshake, very firm for such a tiny woman. She was at least three or four inches shorter than I, which put her under five feet. "I'm Grace Joyner. I spoke with a gentleman about my husband, Harold. He died this morning in the Beaufort hospital, and Middleton's was supposed to pick him up. The man told me to call for an appointment, but I came on over. I don't want there to be any mix-ups. You haven't started embalming him, have you? I *don't* want Harry embalmed."

"Actually, no one is ever embalmed until the next of kin has signed a permission form," I said. "I can assure you that the gentleman you spoke with, Odell Middleton, who is one of the owners and my boss, told me that Mr. Joyner is not to be embalmed. One of our drivers is bringing your husband from the hospital now."

"I'd like to finalize the plans. I want everything green."

Immediately, my mind flashed to an emerald colored casket lined with shiny lime satin. The lady probably didn't want that at all. If she wanted green, she'd most likely choose a muted olive exterior with a soft sea breeze interior. Mentally, I flipped through our catalogs. I couldn't remember ever seeing green caskets. Of course, nowadays, coffins can be custom-made.

A red flag popped up in my thoughts. Mrs. Joyner didn't want her husband embalmed. Probably read too many books about it or watched a video on YouTube. I went to one of those websites last year, but I didn't watch it all the way through. I don't hang out to see Otis or Odell prep bodies either. "Prep" is funeral jargon for "embalm." I work in a mortuary, but my job is to beautify decedents to create beautiful memories for their loved ones.

"Actually, Mrs. Joyner," I said, "arrangements are usually made with one of the Middletons, Otis or Odell. Otis is out sick, but Odell should be back before too late. I could set an appointment for you in a few hours."

She frowned. "I just want to be sure that you don't jump the gun and do anything I don't want. I've driven over here because I want to set everything up, and now you can't do it?" Her tone was more authoritative than disappointed.

"Mrs. Joyner, you and I can discuss the services. The only thing I can't do is name prices. I'll have one of the Middletons call you with a quote."

"That's fine."

I didn't bother to tell her she'd have to come back for payment arrangements before any services were rendered.

"Follow me, please." I led her to a consultation room. "Would you like something to drink?" I asked.

"Yes, herbal tea would be nice. Do you have that?"

"Yes, ma'am. Please excuse me for a few minutes." I went to the kitchen and prepared a tray—a silver tea service with real Wedgwood cups and saucers. Otis insists that coffee or tea be served as his mother did years ago. In the back, we drink from mugs, but they're never seen up front.

When I arrived up front with the tray, we doctored our tea. I took cream and sugar. With the silver tongs, Mrs. Joyner daintily added a slice of lemon to her cup.

I'd sat in with Otis and Odell many times, but this was my first time actually in charge of a planning. This "green" obsession and the woman's attitude made me nervous, but I felt confident I could do it if I just remembered the steps the Middletons used.

An entire set of forms on a clipboard is always available on each conference table. I picked up the papers and the casket book. In South Carolina, mortuaries are required by law to have actual caskets on display, but we use a book of photographs to soften the blow of the selection room and to show special orders. Oops! If Mrs. Joyner didn't want her husband embalmed, I should discourage her from a custom-made unit. Without prepping, Otis and Odell wouldn't want the service delayed any longer than necessary.

We began filling in the top of the first form with personal information. There wasn't much to write. Grace Joyner gave me John Harold Joyner as name of the deceased. When I asked his date of birth, she said, "February 14. We celebrated his birthday on Valentines' Day ever since I met him, but I'm not sure exactly how old he is . . . or should I say 'was'? He always said he was forty-nine." She smiled, then continued, "Of course, I knew better than that."

"What about your marriage certificate?" I suggested. "The year of Mr. Joyner's birth should be on that."

Grace Joyner blushed to the tips of her thick silver bangs.

"Well, truth is Harry and I never married. I know that's surprising for people our age, but I just kinda went over to his house and wound up staying. He took good care of me, and we were happy together."

Pen poised on the form as though the question came from the paper, my next question was plain old nosiness. "How long have you been together?"

"Almost fifteen years, and I admit there were times I wanted to be married, but when I suggested it, Harry always froze and withdrew." She held up her left hand, showing me several carats of diamonds on a matched engagement ring and wedding band. "He bought me these when we were on a cruise, and our friends in Hilton Head just assumed we got married on that trip. We even celebrated our 'anniversary' on the date he bought the rings each year."

Grace Joyner did better with home address and phone numbers. No place of employment for either of them. He'd seen her waiting tables at a grill near his favorite golf course and asked her out. When they got serious, she'd quit work. She assumed that he had retired before she met him.

"I'll have to look for it," she said when I asked for Mr. Joyner's social security number.

"Check with the hospital," I said. "Surely they had it to admit him."

When I asked about life insurance, Mrs. Joyner said, "Harry didn't carry any, but he's left me with more than adequate holdings to pay whatever this costs." She coughed. "We don't have health coverage either. Harry always just paid for anything we needed or wanted."

I didn't tell her that the Middletons would require payment for their services in advance if there were no insurance funds to be assigned. I'd leave that up to Otis or Odell.

Anticipating some problems in obtaining a green casket on short notice, I decided to have her select the coffin before determining time and place of services. Otis would have hissy fits if he knew this. He *always* saved that decision until toward the end of planning sessions.

Otis is generally pickier about things like that, actually about everything, than his brother. He's far more anal-retentive than Odell. If Otis really had the stomach-flu, I'd bet he wasn't as anal-retentive as usual. I was conscious of a quick flush on my cheeks as I squelched the little chuckle at my impolite thought.

"I don't feel like we're communicating," Mrs. Joyner said as she sipped her tea.

"Harry's funeral is to be totally green. The hearse, family cars, gravesite—everything is to be green."

*Why, oh why? My very first time trying to make arrangements by myself with a client, and I got a kook. Did she want us to paint our vehicles?*

"I'm sorry," I said. "I've never heard of a green hearse. I don't know that we could even borrow one." *That would definitely make the Middletons unhappy! They got ticked off everytime I forgot to call it a funeral coach.*

The little woman smiled, then she chuckled. Finally she couldn't contain herself and exploded into uproarious laughter. "Do you think I'm saying I want a casket and hearse that are colored green?" she spluttered.

"Yes, ma'am. Isn't that what you mean?"

"No, the green I'm talking about means environmentally friendly. That's why I decided to bury Harry closer to St. Mary than to Hilton Head. Taylor's Cemetery is the only one I've found that doesn't require a vault or concrete blocks around the coffin. A green funeral is one that allows the body and its container to return to the earth as rapidly as possible. No big vehicles sucking up the earth's resources. If motor vehicles are used, they must be small and gas efficient."

I whooshed out a sigh of relief.

"What kind of casket is a green one then? Wooden?"

"Heaven's no! Those fancy wooden things have metal attachments that will never disintegrate. I want wicker, rattan, or reed with a pure cotton liner and no metal or plastic handles."

"Okay, I'm glad you explained that to me. I'm sure Odell will know about ordering the green casket." That was a bold-face lie. I didn't think he would. Otherwise, he wouldn't have thought a green funeral would be a St. Patrick's Day event, but he'd know how to find out. To be honest, at the moment, I had no idea where to buy a wicker coffin. I wondered if my Gullah friend Rizzie and her brother, who make sweet grass baskets, could weave something big enough to hold a grown man.

"Let me show you our Slumber Rooms," I said.

Mrs. Joyner followed me to Slumber Room A. I motioned toward the giant television screen. "We're now offering video memorials. Supply us with photographs and we create a DVD with background music. It's very comforting and meaningful to play during the visitation."

*Shih tzu! I'd goofed again. A visitation was highly unlikely, maybe even illegal, if the body wasn't being embalmed.*

"I'll think about that. I do have lots of pictures Harry and I took during our travels. Of course, if we have a visitation, it will simply be a celebration of his life with a portrait on an easel. I don't believe in putting the dead person's body on display."

Considering her husband wouldn't be embalmed, I was glad to hear that. And, yes, I realized he wasn't really her husband, but I figured after fifteen years together, she'd earned the title of wife. My marriage had been legal and only lasted three years.

"One reason I wanted to come directly here was to ask if you're familiar with this." She pulled an envelope from her purse and handed it to me. Gold embossed lettering on it read, "Print Memories."

"No, this is new to me."

"Look through the brochure. They make jewelry with your loved one's fingerprints on it. I want a diamond and gold ten-charm bracelet with Harry's fingerprints. Materials for the funeral director to take the prints are in the pocket on the back. I've filled in the forms for what I want, but it has to be ordered through a funeral home. Can you take the prints and send them in?"

"Yes, ma'am. We'll be glad to take care of that." I knew the Middletons would require payment before this left St. Mary, but I could take the prints. When I was a kindergarten teacher, we took our children's prints to make ID's for their parents.

"Well, I'm going to ride out to Taylor's Cemetery and be sure they really offer green burial. I'll call you to see if your boss is back when I finish."

"Yes, ma'am. And Mrs. Joyner, I'm so sorry for your loss. We'll be sure that everything is to your satisfaction."

"Blessed Assurance" accompanied Mrs. Joyner out the front door.

# Chapter Three

Respectfully quiet. That's the ambiance desired in a mortuary. Otis and Odell have told me so many times that I usually remember to maintain calmness at work. The hymns and gospel songs that play over the intercom are soft and peaceful. The atmosphere was tranquil, and the air conditioning was doing an excellent job as I sat at the computer researching green funerals. I almost wet my pants when a loud noise blasted behind the funeral home.

I rushed to the employee door and looked out. The newer funeral coach was backed up to the loading dock. Jake's head was sort of hanging out the open driver's window, and I could see his hand pounding on the horn control. I honestly don't think I'd ever heard the sound of the hearse horn before.

"What's the matter?" I called to Jake.

"I need my epi-pen. A hornet stung me, and I left my medical injector on the seat in my car." He waved toward his rattletrap Chevy parked beside my blue 1966 Mustang. I ran down and opened the door. The pen lay on the seat. By the time I got it back to the hearse window, Jake was gasping. His head jerked and he wheezed what few breaths he took. I yanked the cover off, cocked the pen, and jammed the injector into Jake's arm. His breathing began to improve immediately.

"Can I do anything else?" I asked. "Get you some

water or something to drink?"

"No, it's easing up now. I can't believe I left my epi-pen here. I always keep it in my pocket."

"Was the bee in the funeral coach?"

"It was a hornet, not a bee," Jake answered, "and it must have been in the hearse, because I had the windows rolled up, and I got stung just a block or so from here. If it had gotten me anywhere else, I probably wouldn't have made it."

We generally unload bodies the minute they arrive, and Mr. Joyner should have been no exception. After all, he wasn't going to be embalmed. We needed to get him into cold storage ASAP, but I stood by the vehicle window and talked to Jake until he seemed to be okay. Then we moved Mr. Joyner to the cooler.

"Do you need me to stay here with you, Callie?" Jake asked.

"No, I'll be fine. Odell has gone to take that man we found in the Jaguar to MUSC, and Otis is home sick, but the only client is Mr. Joyner. His wife wants a green funeral, so we won't be embalming him. All I'll really be doing until Odell returns is answering the telephone." *And playing on the Internet or reading a book,* I thought.

"A green funeral?" Jake asked.

"Yes, I've just been reading about it on the Internet. A green funeral is ecologically friendly to the earth and our environment. No gas-hog vehicles, no markers meant to last forever. Instead, they plant a tree or wildflowers in memory of the deceased."

"Why don't they embalm? Religious beliefs?"

"No, they just believe the body should disintegrate into the earth ASAP. They use biodegradable caskets too."

"What the heck is a biodegradable casket?" Jake almost laughed. "I guess they don't want anything made of Styrofoam."

"I guess not," I said. "They want coffins made of materials that will decompose rapidly. Some are hardly more than cardboard, but there are a lot of basket types available made of woven wicker or reed. Want to come in and see them on the computer?"

"No, after an episode, I need to rest for a while. I'm going home. My mom will probably make me go to the doctor, but if you need me, call, and I'll try to come back."

After Jake left, I returned to the computer. I assumed that Otis and Odell would be pleasantly surprised. I'd found and printed out numerous sites dealing with wicker and reed casket suppliers. One thing that confused me was that Mrs. Joyner had said she was checking with Taylor's Cemetery, but the articles I'd been reading indicated that green funerals were limited to only a few specified graveyards.

In the midst of pondering that Mrs. Joyner wouldn't want a gravestone or marker, I remembered that she had mentioned a memorial. She wanted jewelry with her husband's fingerprints on it. I picked up the brochure she'd left with me and read about all the possibilities. They offered silver as well as 14-carat yellow gold and platinum. Each piece was custom-made, and the prints could become a part of a ring, a pendant, a brooch, tie tack—almost anything imaginable. The brochure also listed what the mortician needed to do and send to the manufacturer for each project. Prices weren't quoted. Funeral directors were instructed to call for prices before sending in the prints, orders, and payments. No CODs either.

Mrs. Joyner's choice of the gold charm bracelet with diamonds looked like one of the more expensive items and meant that all ten fingers needed to be printed. The ink pad and cards for a full set of prints were included in the packet. I manicure dead hands as part of my job, so taking prints from a corpse wasn't distasteful. Then I thought about forensics technicians who sometimes peel a cadaver's hand and slip their own hand into the skin glove to make fingerprints when putrefaction has already begun. Now, that's something I didn't want to do.

I'd assumed Mr. Joyner died recently at the hospital, and Jake and I had managed to get him chillin' in our cooler before Jake left, but I decided the sooner I took care of this assignment, the better. I pulled on a pair of latex gloves, picked up the kit, and went through the prep rooms to the cold storage area.

Otis took me to visit a mortuary once that had an actual refrigerated room where bodies were out in the open on gurneys. Our set-up was more like the morgues on television, only smaller. Decedents were placed on stainless steel trays that slid into chilled slots. I pulled Mr. Joyner from his space.

Okay, I could have taken the prints by just unzipping the body bag and pulling his hands through the opening. For some reason, I didn't do it that way. I unzipped the bag and laid it open exposing the body. Earlier that day, I'd called a white-haired man an old geezer, with no reason at all. That wouldn't happen here. "Gentleman" was obviously the correct term for him.

Clothed in expensive navy blue pajamas with cream-colored cording on the collar and cuffs, the man was obviously in his seventies, maybe even eighties, but his body was trim and toned. His skin looked healthy—tanned with hardly a wrinkle—and his hair was perfectly coiffed salt and pepper gray. Now, how could his hair be so perfect after he'd died and been hauled to a funeral home? I touched it. A very firm-hold hair spray. I wondered if he'd died with it looking that way or someone had styled it after death. *What killed him? He had none of the marks or signs of resuscitation efforts. He looked as though he'd just gone to sleep—a handsome, well-cared for older man in his neatly pressed PJ's.* He did, however, smell—not like death or the frequent scent when the bowels loosen at death. He smelled of garlic. I must have been so worried about Jake when we brought him in that I didn't notice it. If he'd smelled like almonds, I would have suspected poison, but I'd never read about a poison that smelled like garlic.

I lifted Mr. Joyner's hand. The nails were professionally manicured and buffed. The fingers were stiff. I slid the pajama sleeve up to his elbow. The underside of his arm was a deep, mottled pink. Livor mortis. Discoloration of the skin caused by the drainage and settling of blood in the bottom parts of the body after death.

Opening the ink pad and laying out the rigid paper for the fingerprints, I thought it might be easier to get the prints with the fingers so stiff. The first attempt disproved that theory. It might have been easier to roll an inflexible finger if it weren't attached to a full hand of other unmovable fingers. After a couple of tries, I decided that unless I was prepared to remove the fingers from the hand—ugh—I'd be ahead to loosen the rigor. I methodically massaged and thumped each finger until they were all flexible. After that, the fingerprints were a breeze. Ten clear, sharp prints—each in its properly labeled space on the cards.

I cleaned his fingers, zipped the body bag closed, and returned Mr. Joyner and his tray to its assigned place, then I hurried toward my office with the print cards.

"Jesus Loves Me" sounded. Someone had entered the front door. I hurried to the foyer and met Sheriff Harmon.

"Callie, I've come to take your statement about this morning." He held up a pocket recorder.

"Okay, let's do it in the conference room here." I motioned toward the same room I'd been in earlier with Mrs. Joyner.

I put the print cards on the table beside his little

recorder. "What do you want to know?" I asked.

The sheriff flipped the device on, then recorded the date, time, location, and that he, Wayne Corley, Sheriff of Jade County, was interviewing Calamine Lotion Parrish. I grimaced when he said that. My name really *is* Calamine Lotion, but the only person who calls me that is the man who laid that name on me—my daddy. My mother died right after I was born. Daddy was so upset that he got drunk, really drunk, and named me the only pink thing he could think of—Calamine Lotion. I've thought many a time how glad I was he didn't consider Pepto Bismol.

It didn't take long to answer Sheriff Harmon's questions. "All I know is that the man looked asleep, but when that fly crawled around on his nose, I got scared and tried to wake him. Finelay Best broke the window. I felt the body and determined he was dead."

"How did you know he was dead?" Sheriff Harmon asked. "I would assume he wasn't breathing and his heart wasn't beating, but you didn't have any way to check brain function."

I laughed. I promise, I didn't mean to laugh, but I did. "Folks can argue criteria for dead all they want," I said. "Brain death, heart death, whatever, but I didn't need a mirror to hold under that man's nose to check to see if he was dead. Rigor mortis had set in."

"What about the snake?" the sheriff asked. "Did you see the snake?"

"No," I answered. "I didn't, but Best swore he saw an Eastern Coral snake in the car. Your new deputy, Blake, arrived, and right after that, you were there."

"Had you ever seen this man before?" Sheriff Harmon asked.

"Who? Blake?" I asked. "He's new, isn't he? This morning's the first time I've seen him."

"Yeah, he hasn't been with the department long.

Moved down here from Philadelphia. But I was asking if you'd ever seen the dead man before."

"Never before today." I paused. "Was there really a snake in the car?" I asked.

"Now, Callie, you know that I ask and you answer," Harmon said.

I cut him an *oh, you meannie* look. I grew up with Wayne Harmon hanging around our house because he was friends with my five older brothers. He finally smiled and said, "But I don't guess it hurts to tell you that yes, we found a fairly young Eastern coral in the car, about twenty-inches long, down under the straw seat protector the man was sitting on."

"Do you know his name? Where he's from? What was he doing here?" I asked, running all my questions together and meaning, of course, the man, not the snake.

"ID in his wallet says he's Richard Arthur and that he lived in Hilton Head. I've got people trying to contact a wife or relative, but they haven't found anyone yet."

"Do you think the snake killed him?"

"Won't know until the autopsy results. There did appear to be a gnawed place on the underside of his thigh. That could have been where the coral snake got him. If so, the cause of death could be venom."

Sheriff Harmon stood up. "If you think of anything else, give me a call." He grinned then sang to the tune of an old country song my daddy sometimes sings, "And, Callie, I can handle this job all by myself."

I walked the sheriff to the front, grateful that the music changes each time the door opens or closes. I get teary-eyed each time "Jesus Loves Me" plays. Makes me think about prepping and burying babies. Instead, a soft version of "Immortal, Invisible, God Only Wise" lifted my spirits from thoughts of children dying.

*Dalmation!* My print cards were missing when I went

back to the conference room. Perhaps they'd fallen on the floor. I was on my hands and knees searching the carpet under the table when Odell came in.

"What are you doing under there? Did you lose a contact lens or something?" Odell growled.

"No, I don't even wear lenses. I put some fingerprint cards on this table, and now I can't find them." I backed out from under the table and stood.

"Fingerprints? For what?" he asked.

"Mrs. Joyner came by. She brought this brochure and kit for Memory Prints." I picked up the package and handed it to him."

"Yes, I've seen this at conventions."

"Well, Mrs. Joyner wants a gold charm bracelet with her husband's prints. Since he won't be embalmed, I went ahead and took the fingerprints when Jake brought Mr. Joyner in."

"Good." Odell flipped through the brochure. "Have you contacted this company yet to see what our cost is on this?"

"Not yet."

"Have there been any other calls?"

"No. Mr. Joyner is the only one here."

"I don't guess Doofus has phoned."

"No, I haven't heard from Otis."

"He said he'd let us know if he felt better and decided to come in. He sounded pretty bad this morning though." Odell set the brochure back on the table. "Do you want to go to lunch first?"

"No," I replied, knowing that the question meant he was ready to go himself.

"Shall I bring you something or do you want to go out when I get back?"

"Just bring me a sandwich, please." I looked around the room. "I can't imagine what happened to those cards.

I assume it's okay that I had to break the rigor in Mr. Joyner's fingers to roll them on the paper."

"No problem, but next time, try rolling the paper against the finger. If you don't find the cards, you can ask for another kit when you call about prices."

"Okay. We don't know yet when Mrs. Joyner wants him buried, and we're going to have to order the special casket she wants."

"What kind of special?"

"Ecologically friendly. I've checked the Internet, and they're available here in South Carolina, near Charlotte, so the worse scenario will be sending someone to pick up whatever she decides on. They're biodegradable, and most of them are cardboard or baskets like wicker or reed."

"Yeah, I've seen those at conventions, too, but that didn't cross my mind when she said 'green'. What time is she coming back?"

"She's gone to Taylor's Cemetery and will call when she's finished there. I told her she'd have to wait until you came back for prices."

"Well, I shouldn't be gone more than an hour, and the sooner we set everything up, the better. Schedule her for anytime this afternoon." He started toward the door, then turned back toward me. "And where is Jake? We may have to send him to pick up the basket."

"He was stung by a hornet. Thank heaven he was almost back to the funeral home because he'd left his epi-pen in his car."

"Did you call an ambulance?"

"No, I gave him the injection, and he seemed okay, but he said he was going home, maybe to the doctor."

"We'll work it out. First things first," Odell said. I thought he was talking about Mrs. Joyner selecting the casket before we worried about picking it up. However, being Odell, he added as he left, "The first thing for me is to get some lunch. I'm starving."

I'd barely settled back at my desk when the telephone rang. "Middleton's Mortuary. This is Callie. How may I help you?" I said, expecting the caller to be Mrs. Joyner.

"Ohhhhhh, Callie, this is Jane." Like I wouldn't recognize Jane's voice, even full of tears. After all, she *is* my best friend, and presently my roommate, until they finish replacing the carpet in my apartment and I move back next door.

"What's wrong?" I asked. Couldn't be a family emergency. Jane had no family. Her daddy ran off when her blindness was discovered in her infancy, and her mother died right after Jane and I graduated from high school.

"It's your brother!" she sniffled. I have five brothers, whom I call The Boys because I don't think they'll ever grow up, but no need to ask which one Jane was talking about. She was engaged to marry Frank in December. Another brother, Bill, was supposed to marry his long-time, on again, off again girlfriend Molly in a few weeks. John, my favorite, most genteel brother, lives in Atlanta and had what I thought was the perfect marriage until he told me he was considering leaving his wife.

So far as my other two brothers, Mike and Jim, are concerned, each has a marriage and divorce in his past. Like me, I don't think either has recovered from the first go-round enough to consider slipping a gold band on anyone else's hand. Personally, I don't know that I ever want to remarry. Divorcing Donnie kind of spoiled the whole romantic notion to me, and the only real thing I got out of it was my vintage Mustang, which was Donnie's pride and joy, and a less than healthy fear of becoming too involved or vulnerable with anyone.

Back to Jane, on the phone, sobbing.

"What did he do?" I asked her.

"He wants to move our marriage up to October and

have a double wedding with Bill and Molly." She was now bawling like a cow at milking time.

"What's wrong with that?" I asked.

"I don't want to get married so soon, and besides, if we do that, everything has to be the way Molly's planned it. I don't want a big, fancy reception. I can't afford it either, and Frank says he'll pay for our part, but if his bank account is flush, why's he living with your daddy?"

"I don't know a thing about Frank's income," I answered, but I didn't think he'd have money to pay for half of the shindig Molly was planning. Besides, the invitations for Bill and Molly's wedding had been sent a month ago.

"What kind of wedding do you want?" I asked.

"Just you as my maid of honor and Frank having one of his brothers stand for him. A simple church wedding with cake and punch afterwards in the fellowship hall."

"That sure sounds better than all that folderol Donnie's mother insisted on when we were married. Donnie's family paid for a lot of it, but it was a waste of money for my daddy as well as their family."

"What should I tell Frank?"

"Tell him that he's already had a wedding, but this is your first and that as the bride, it should be the way you want it."

"Had *a* wedding? Can't you keep your brothers straight? Frank's been married twice already."

"You're right. Even more reason to let you plan it."

The sniffles stopped. "I'll just tell him what you said." She paused. "When will you be home? I'm cooking dinner."

"I don't know. I'll call you when I leave here. I was supposed to work from one this afternoon until eight tonight, but I got called in early."

"Who died?"

"Nobody you know. Two old men. Kinda unusual. They're both from Hilton Head."

"Do you think—" Call waiting beeped in and caller ID showed a call from H Joyner. "Gotta go, Jane. This is a business call. We'll talk tonight."

I hit "flash" and answered, "Middleton's Mortuary. Callie speaking. How may I help you?"

# Chapter Four

Odell sat with Grace Joyner and me at the conference table. I'd barely had time to scarf down the barbecue sandwich Odell brought me for lunch before the widow arrived. She was over half an hour earlier than we'd scheduled on the phone. Appointments didn't seem to mean a lot to Mrs. Joyner.

Although Odell isn't as polished as Otis, he's a much smoother speaker during a funeral planning session than at other times. He'd explained to Mrs. Joyner, "We don't stock any 'green' caskets and there are none in our catalog, but Ms. Parrish here has printed out several options from the computer."

"Several" was an understatement. Basket caskets as I thought of them, came in many types of materials—wicker, and rattan for starters. Manufactured primarily in England and China, they could be traditional coffin-shaped—wider at the top for the shoulders, narrowing as the basket reached the foot area. They could be completely rectangular like the most popular American caskets these days. Corners could be squared or rounded. Colored bands of rattan or ribbon were sometimes woven into the sides.

"What's this?" Grace Joyner asked and touched one of the photographs.

The one she'd indicated had a divided lid so that the

top half could be opened without the bottom. "That's called the American Viewing Model," I replied.

"I know I don't want that," she said. "I don't believe in putting dead people on display."

Okay, I admit that her comment kinda hurt my feelings. My *job* is to make the deceased look good for viewing.

"Another option," Odell offered, "would be cremation."

"Oh, no," the tiny woman shuddered as she spoke. I wondered why she'd be so opposed to cremation. After all, she wasn't into preserving the body. Why not just speed it up all the way? Her answer came quickly.

"Do you realize that crematories use tremendous amounts of energy resources to produce the necessary heat?" she asked. "Not only that, but cremation releases pollution into the air. It's definitely not an acceptable alternative to green or natural burial."

Odell looked a little confused, then recovered. "Certainly, we'll be happy to handle Mr. Joyner's services however you like."

Grace Joyner looked through the papers again. She kept returning to the same page, then held it out to Odell.

"This is what I want," she said.

Odell took the paper and read aloud. Mrs. Joyner had selected "a traditional shaped willow unit in weatherbeaten gold color with green bands inlaid into the sides, woven handles, and unbleached white cotton liner."

I leafed through the computer print-outs Odell set back on the table and found the one for the closest supplier. "If you'll excuse me," I said, "I'll step into the office and see how soon we can have this delivered."

At my office desk, I called the nearest dealer, who didn't stock that model. The next closest was located in North Carolina, about four and a half to five hours away from St. Mary.

The gentleman who answered the telephone identified himself as Al Harper. After I read the casket description to him, he said, "Yes, we've got one like that in stock. It's made in England, but it's a pretty popular choice, so I keep a few on hand. What size do you need?"

"He's an average sized adult male, neither extremely tall nor heavy."

"No problem. Shall we ship it?"

When I'd first come to work for the Middletons, I would have said, "Certainly."

Now I knew that whenever possible, Otis and Odell preferred to pick up anything within a reasonable drive. We'd had too many slip-ups during the several years I'd been working at the funeral home. Occasionally a casket wasn't shipped when promised, and at other times, it would arrive on schedule but not be the exact model we'd ordered.

"How late are you open?" I asked.

"I'll be here until six, but I can give you my cell number. Call when you get to town. I'll meet you whatever time you arrive."

When I returned to the conference room, I assured Mrs. Joyner that we could have the casket in St. Mary this evening, no later than early the next morning.

"Great!" she said. "Then let's plan the burial for early tomorrow afternoon."

"And Taylor's Cemetery assured you there would be no problem about burying without a liner or vault?" Odell asked.

"They said no problem and accepted my money for a plot," she answered. "The man said that the graveyard is so old that many of the graves are unlined. They fill in settling of the earth whenever necessary." She smiled. "They'll let me plant a tree instead of placing a monument, too. I plan to pick up a crape myrtle tree from the nursery this afternoon. Some of them blossom all summer, and since fall is so late settling in this year, the manager said he has several still in bloom. The planting will be part of the service."

"When I was reading about environmentally friendly funerals, they mentioned planting trees and suggested burial in woodlands instead of cemeteries," I commented.

"Yes, but in my case, I don't own any woodlands. I'd like for Harry to be close enough to home for me to come visit his tree sometimes, but not so near that I'd be tempted to sit by his grave every day. There's not a commercial woodlands burial park near here."

The telephone rang, and I excused myself to answer it while Odell finished with Mrs. Joyner's plans and financial arrangements.

"Middleton's Mortuary. Callie speaking. How may I help you?"

"Callie, I've decided not to cook." Jane wasn't crying anymore. "I'm so angry with your brother that I don't want to *be* here if he comes over. I'll be dressed when you get home. I'll treat you to dinner anywhere you like that isn't too expensive."

"Fine," I answered, "but I'm hoping Odell will send me to pick up a casket this afternoon. It's almost a five-hour drive to North Carolina and five hours back. I'll get overtime. Do you want to go if he sends me?"

"I'd like to, but Roxanne needs to work tonight. Frank's been over here so much lately that I'm way off on hours this month. You know I don't work when he's around. Guess I'll have to pass."

Roxanne is Jane's "professional" name. She calls her job "fantasy acting," but to call a spade a flippin' shovel, Jane works on a 900 sex phone line. As Roxanne, she sweet-talks men. It sounds negative, but she makes good money and doesn't have to pay for transportation to and from work. Her hours are flexible, and there's only been one time that she recognized the voice of one of her customers other than on the telephone.


As I slid under the steering wheel of the hearse (ex-scuuze me, the funeral coach), Odell leaned in and said, "You'll need your cell phone to call the owner to meet you. Do you have it with you and is it charged? It's three now, so it'll be about eight o'clock by the time you get there." He harrumphed.

I held my cell phone up for him to see. "It was on charge all night," I assured him.

"I'd really rather not send you on a ten-hour trip, but with Otis sick and Jake not well, it's one or the other of us. I want to be nearby in case Otis needs me. Are you sure you don't mind?"

"I'm positive. Besides, I'm not going by myself. Jane called back. She's riding with me."

"Wait a minute," Odell said and went over to his Buick. He pulled something from his glove compartment and brought it back to me. He handed over a pearl-handled snub-nosed .22 revolver.

"Just in case," he growled. "If you have any trouble, call 911, then me. I'll feel more comfortable if you have this with you." He added, "It was my mother's and it's loaded, but the safety is on."

I slipped the gun into the glove compartment of the funeral coach. I grew up with a redneck dad and five older brothers who all hunted. I'm not scared of guns, and I know how to use them.

Jane's apartment is the other side of the duplex I usually live in. My place was bloodied up a while back, and I was getting a fresh paint job and new carpeting, so I'd been staying with Jane. When I opened the door and called out, "Jane, it's me," Big Boy, my Great Dane came bounding over with his leash in his mouth.

Blindness doesn't interfere with Jane's capabilities. She and Big Boy had overcome their problem. When the three of us first started staying together, Jane didn't always know when he needed to go out. He'd bring the leash to her, which was his signal he needed a potty break. Jane would scratch his back, unable to see the leash. They'd worked it out by Big Boy yipping at her and dropping his leash in her lap when he wanted out. Apparently, they weren't communicating well this afternoon because Big Boy looked at me with an expression that said, "My eyes are floating. Get me outside before I burst."

As always, he ran to the scraggly oak at the corner of the yard. One of these days, my doggie will lift his leg on that tree. He's over a year old now, and he still doesn't tee tee like a boy dog. That's not the funniest part of it. He "hides" behind the tree, not realizing that both his head and his hind quarters are visible on either side of the tree trunk while he modestly squats and relieves himself like a girl dog.

"Come on, Big Boy," I called when he'd finished and began sniffing around the yard. He followed me back into the apartment.

"Why don't we take him with us?" Jane asked.

"Because I don't want him slobbering and shedding hair all over the funeral coach," I answered as I filled his water bowl and poured Kibbles 'n Bits into the food bowl.

"Oh, I didn't know we were taking the hearse," Jane said.

"How did you think we could bring back a casket in my Mustang?" I asked as I locked up the apartment and led Jane to the passenger side.

"I don't know. You said it's made of straw. I guess I

thought maybe it folded up." She slammed the door, and I went around to the driver's side. We were on I-95 headed toward Charleston before I finished explaining that the casket was woven like a giant basket big enough to hold an adult, but not made out of straw.

"Did you bring me a Dr Pepper?" Jane asked. She's really not too interested in the mortuary or anything to do with it.

"No, we'll stop somewhere for drinks and supper, too."

When we'd made the giant turn off I-95 onto I-26 toward Columbia, I'd decided to eat early, but Jane had gone to sleep. Since she won't be reading this, I can say that she snores. Loud and long. I didn't want to wake her, so I just barreled along the highway playing the radio and listening to Cousin Roger on WXYW.

"Call in now," he said. "Be the seventh caller and have your name entered into the 'Thankful for Love' contest. The winning couple will have an all-expenses-paid wedding and honeymoon on Thanksgiving weekend, paid for by Happy Jack's Campground. Get your name in the pot now!"

Jane was asleep. My cell phone lay on the seat between us. I snatched it up and entered the number Cousin Roger had given. I squealed when I heard, "You are caller number seven. Turn your radio down and give us your name, please." I'm not even dating anyone. What am I going to do with a wedding?

"This is Jane Baker," I lied.

"Okay, Jane, we're going to put you and your fiancée in for the grand prize. What's the lucky man's name?"

"Uh, Frank, Frank Parrish," I said.

"All right, Jane. Now hold on because I'm going to get your address and phone number while this next song plays."

Sure enough, Gene Holdway's version of "Sweet Suzanne" played softly on the radio while I gave Jane's home address and telephone number to Cousin Roger. When I disconnected the call, I squealed so loud that Jane woke up.

"Wha . . . what's wrong?" she sputtered.

"I just got you and Frank entered for an all-expense-paid wedding and honeymoon in November. It's a radio contest, and I was the seventh caller."

"You won?" she screeched even louder than I had.

"No, but you're in the finals."

"I'm also in the finals for a bathroom break real soon," she said and squirmed in her seat.

"I'll get off at the next exit. I could use a break plus I'm getting hungry."

We pulled off at one of the Orangeburg exits, filled the tank on Middleton's gas credit card, and went into Aeden's Café. After a quick trip to their restroom, we ordered Calabash style chicken plates and pigged out, food compliments of Middleton's Visa. When we returned to the hearse, Jane snuggled up in the corner and was soon snoring again. So much for bringing her along for company.

Normally, I'd think she'd been up all night talking on the 900 telephone sex line as Roxanne, the "fantasy actress." I didn't think Roxanne had worked the night before though because Frank had been there with Jane when I went to bed. Jane didn't work when Frank was at the apartment. He knew how she earned a living, but he wanted her to quit the job. Jane had refused, maintaining that she did nothing wrong and that she made enough money on that hot line to support herself. She had agreed to find different work once they were married.

In Columbia, we switched from I-26 to I-20 and then a few miles later onto I-77 toward Charlotte, North

Carolina. That would take us directly to Tanner, just south of Charlotte. By the time we reached the North Carolina state line, I was sleepy myself. I exited at one of those places where the Interstate sign showed only one brand of gas available. Nothing in the way of food or lodging. I pulled in beside the little concrete block filling station, not wanting to obstruct their two gas pumps just because I hoped they had fresh coffee.

"Where are we?" Jane asked as she sat up when we stopped.

"Just taking a coffee break," I said.

As Jane turned, she bumped the latch on the glove compartment. It flopped open and she fumbled around to close it. "Careful," I said. "There's a loaded gun in there."

"What?" Jane demanded.

"Odell insisted we bring it in case we break down on the way and anyone bothers us."

"Anybody bothers us, I'll beat 'em to death with my cane."

"Yeah, if you ever wake up. I thought you came along to keep me company."

"I'm just tired. Frank and I stayed up arguing most of the night."

"Maybe you need to rethink this marriage business."

"I'm thinking the same thing while you're calling in winning us a wedding."

"You haven't won yet. Let me get some us coffee. We'll talk the rest of the ride. Put that gun away." She put it in the glove compartment and slammed it closed.

"Are we still in South Carolina?" Jane asked.

"No, we've passed the state line."

"Somebody told me if you carry a gun in North Carolina, it has to be out in the open."

"Do you really think the law lets you carry a loaded gun on the seat in North Carolina?"

"Well, you don't even know if carrying it in the glove compartment is legal in South Carolina. That's a concealed weapon. I think it's supposed to be locked up in the trunk."

"A hearse doesn't have a trunk."

"Are we at the gas pump?" Jane asked as she opened her door and stepped out.

"No, I parked by the side of the building. I'm supposed to fill up the hearse only on Middleton's gas charge card, and this is the wrong brand. We don't need more fuel yet anyway, so I pulled away from the front."

# Chapter Five

Guiding Jane into the store, I noticed it looked even smaller on the inside and had a little pot-bellied stove in the middle of the floor. The air was cooler up here than in St. Mary, but not cold enough for a fire. Bread and a few canned goods stocked the mostly bare shelves. A chubby young woman with a dark brown pony tail sat on a stool behind the counter. She was shelling and eating boiled peanuts. When she looked up and saw us, she scraped the shells off the counter into a trash can, then tore a few paper towels from the roll by the register and wiped her hands and lips. She popped two pieces of chewing gum in her mouth. Her name tag identified her as Betty Jo.

"Do you have fresh coffee and can we use your restroom?" I asked.

"Yeah, I just made the coffee a while ago, and the law makes us let you use the bathroom. It's back there." I wondered, *Would Betty Jo make us wet our underpants if the law didn't require a public restroom in the store?* She pointed to a hand-lettered sign that read JOHN at the back of the store. "It's unisex," she called as Jane and I headed that way, "so be sure to lock the door."

"I don't sense a lot of people in here," Jane whispered.

"There's no one except us and Betty Jo," I whispered back.

When I opened the bathroom door, Jane whacked her

mobility cane against the commode and sat before I even got the light switch flipped up. I am constantly amazed at how well she manages.

"Tell me what the clerk looks like," she said when she stood and began her hand washing ritual. Jane has this thing about her hands, and when she washes them, she scrubs up like a surgeon.

"She's young," I answered, "and chubby."

"Chubby or fat?" Jane asked.

"Well, she's a really big girl, on the other side of thick. I guess the truth is she's fat.

"She's chewing gum, isn't she?" Jane asked as she began drying her hands.

"How'd you know that?" I asked, balanced over the commode. I never sit on public toilet seats.

"I could hear her popping gum."

"And," I added, "she chews with her mouth open, too."

"Think she'd know what the gun laws are in North Carolina?" Jane asked.

"I don't know. Let's find out."

The store was still empty when Jane and I came out of the restroom. We walked over to the coffee station, and I poured two cups of high-test—never decaf when we'd be up past midnight. Of course, Jane was used to staying up all night talking on the phone as Roxanne. On the evenings she wasn't Roxanne, it sounded to me in my room as though she and Frank didn't go to bed too early when he stayed over. Ex-cuuze me. They went to bed, but they weren't sleeping. Those sounds I heard from Jane's room definitely weren't snores.

I wasn't totally comfortable with the situation between my brother and my best friend. I love them both, but I know their faults too well. This made me aware that their relationship might not work out, which would result in each of them thinking I should side with one against the other. Also, it was awkward to have my brother spending the night with my roommate. Not that we actually shared a *room*, but we were occupying the same apartment. Since I was staying in *her* side of the duplex until the workers finished in mine, I'd decided just to put my pillow over my head and try to ignore them. I'd be back in my own place soon anyway.

I creamed and sugared the coffees and walked to the register. I handed Jane her cup while I dug around in the bottom of my purse for money. The change accumulated in my handbag seemed to weigh a ton.

"Ask her about the gun," Jane whispered.

"We've got a gun," I said and motioned toward Jane. "My friend wants me to tell you about it."

Betty Jo's hazel eyes widened into big eyes— SpongeBob SquarePants big. She stepped back from the register, stumbled, and caught herself on the shelf behind her.

"Don't get upset," I quickly added. "It's outside—"

"Do you want me to go get it and show it to you?" Jane interrupted.

"No! No! Take what you wanna," the girl screamed. "I can't believe I'm being robbed by a blind woman." She yanked the cash register drawer open. "You can have all the money. Get some cigarettes and beer, soda, anything you want. Just doan hurt me. You doan need to bring the gun in."

Betty Jo reached under the counter, and for a moment, I feared she was pulling a weapon on *us*. Instead, she plopped a pink and orange striped tote bag beside the register. "You can take my pocket book, too." Her whole body shook, and tears streamed down her face, leaving dark streaks of mascara on her round cheeks.

My sometimes wandering mind remembered a line

from *T'was The Night Before Christmas.* The one about the
"little round belly shook like a bowl full of jelly."

"No, no," I said in my most soothing, comforting
mortuary voice. "We don't intend to rob you. We—"

"Kidnap me? You're goan kidnap me," the girl
screamed. We could see sweat popping out on her face
and arms. Well, I could see it. Jane, of course, saw nothing.

"No," I continued, "we're not going to kidnap you,
rob you, or hurt you. We just want to know what the gun
laws are in North Carolina. Should we keep the gun in the
glove compartment or on the seat?"

"I doan know. I din't even finish high school. I doan
know nothin' about gun laws." She picked up the roll of
paper towels, tore off a handful, and wiped her face. "My
daddy," she added, "carries guns in the trunk of the car or
in his truck's gun rack."

"That doesn't help us," Jane said. "This is just a little
handgun, so it wouldn't fit on a gun rack. Besides, the
hearse doesn't have a trunk or a gun rack. Are you sure
you don't want to see the gun?"

"Noooooooooawww!" the girl screeched again and
doubled over as far as her round jelly belly would let her.
For a moment, I was scared she suffered from my malady.
When I'm frightened, I vomit. The last thing I wanted was
to make this girl throw up all over her purse and cash
register.

"Jane," I said firmly, "Betty Jo doesn't want to see the
gun. She doesn't want us to bring it in."

"Hearse? A hearse?" the girl managed to splutter out.
"You're driving a hearse with a gun in it. You problee
would let this blind woman shoot me. You women are
craz—" Her eyes bugged again and she burst into fresh
tears. "I din't mean it," she cried. "I din't mean to call you
crazy, and I doan wanna know why you're ridin' in a
hearse."

"We didn't mean to scare you," I tried to assure her. "Let me just pay for the coffees, and we'll be on our way."

"No, no, no, the coffee's on the house. Just take it." Betty Jo waved her pudgy arm and pointed toward the door.

"We don't mind paying," I said.

"Please, just go," she said.

Jane followed me with one hand clutching the back of my dress and the other holding her coffee. She had her cane tucked under her arm. I noticed movement in the lot. I was glad we'd gotten all this straight before another customer came in.

As we opened the door, a man entered, and I almost heaved myself. He had a do-rag tied around the bottom of his face like a bandit in an old cowboy movie, and he pointed a semi-automatic 9mm hand gun in my face.

"Stop, Jane," I said just as she ran into me, slopping her coffee down the back of my dress. Thank heaven the java wasn't from McDonald's and it wasn't very hot.

"Why?" Jane asked.

"Because she said to," the man snapped. A T-shirt and jeans hung loosely from his skinny frame, and no, he didn't have dreadlocks or a pony tail. His blond high and tight hair cut and pale blue eyes showed above the do-rag.

"What's wrong now?" Betty Jo called. I guessed that Jane and I were blocking the masked man and his firearm from her view.

"You're being robbed!" the man snarled sarcastically.

"No, it's a misunderstanding," Betty Jo said. "They're not robbin' me. They just have a gun."

"A gun?" the robber gasped. He grabbed me around the neck and pressed the pistol barrel right behind my ear. I dropped my cup. Coffee splattered all over the worn, wooden floor.

I tried, I promise I tried, but I couldn't control it. I

retched, and partially digested salad and Calabash fried chicken shot out from my mouth. Some of it landed on the floor and some on the front of my dress. Unfortunately, a tiny bit wound up on the robber's shoes. It smelled like honey mustard.

"What tha . . . ?" the robber spat out and gagged. The *barf-a-rama* scene in Stephen King's *Stand by Me* flashed through my mind.

*Please, God,* I prayed silently, *if he throws up, let him drop the gun first.* I didn't want to be shot, but I especially didn't want to be shot and then covered with some outlaw's vomit.

I have to hand it to that Betty Jo. Still shaking and crying, she grabbed the roll of paper towels and brought them around the counter, tearing off sheets as she came. She looked at me. She looked at the robber. She looked back and forth between our faces. His was furious. She bent and cleaned his shoes, then she tossed those towels into the trash can and tore off more pieces. She wiped off my mouth and dabbed at the front of my dress. Robber man still held the gun barrel against my head.

"What's going on?" Jane demanded.

"Just be still. Don't move at all," I said. "This man *is* robbing the store, and he has a gun aimed at me."

Betty Jo unrolled more paper towels and dropped a handful onto the floor over my chicken and salad. She went back to the still-open drawer of the register and began thrusting very short stacks of money into a plastic grocery bag. She handed the sack and her pink and orange purse to the man. He shoved the gun into his pocket and grabbed the bags.

"Now I want your car keys," he told her.

"I doan have a car," Betty Jo wailed. "My mama brings me to work and picks me up when my shift is over."

"Then gimme yours," the robber said to me.

I handed the funeral coach keys to him. "Where's it parked?" he asked.

"Around on the side," I said, pointing.

"Do I need to shoot you girls or lock you in the cooler or can you wait fifteen minutes before you call the cops? I promise you if you call before then, I'll come back and get you."

The three of us babbled assurances that we wouldn't call anyone. I think Betty Jo promised "forever."

Robber man ran out the door. Betty Jo grabbed Jane and me in a group hug while we laughed and cried at the same time.

Our relief was short-lived. The robber flung the door open and stomped back in, rage on his face and gun pointed at me again.

"There's no car out there. The only thing is a hearse!" he snarled.

"Yeah, that's what we're riding in, dummy," Jane smarted off.

"Shhhhh," I said, "Jane, he has a pistol pointed at me." Then I turned toward the robber. "I gave you the keys," I said calmly. "Take that. It drives just like a car, only it's a little longer. It's got automatic transmission and a CD player."

"Woman, you are out of your mind! I'm not driving a hearse. It's dark outside. No telling what's in the back of that thing."

"There's nothing in the back," Jane said. "We haven't picked up the casket yet."

"I'm not taking any chances," he said.

"I told you it's empty," Jane argued.

"He's talking about ghosts," I said.

"There's no such thing as ghosts," Jane said, then waved her arms and howled out a long, creepy

"Whooooo-oooooooooo." She laughed, and I elbowed her. I guess if a person can't see the gun, it's easier to be brave, or maybe *stupid* is a better word.

"I could call my mama to bring you her car," Betty Jo said.

"I'm not crazy enough to let you call the cops and then sit here 'til they show up."

The man's face contorted from one expression to another—from fear to rage to confusion and back again.

"This ain't going right," he said. "I gotta good mind to go out there and shoot up that hearse."

"No, pul-lease," I said in a disgustingly sugary southern belle tone. "I've already totaled one of the funeral home's family cars. Please don't trash the hearse. Steal it or leave it, but don't shoot holes in it."

"Just shut up!" robber man said. "I need to think. I want all of you over there in front of the counter." He shoved me away from him. "Stand still and be quiet. I gotta figure out what to do."

"Why don't you just leave in the car you came in?" Jane suggested.

"Cause I walked here from where the last car I stole broke down, Miss Smarty Pants!"

Anyone besides Jane, I might have seen a change in the expression in her eyes. Jane's eyes don't look de-formed or strange, but they don't reveal much either. Her face showed nothing, but her entire body tensed, and I knew something was about to happen.

"I don't understand where you want us to stand," Jane said. "Where are Callie and Betty Jo?"

"Behind you," robber man said. "I'll show you." He stepped toward Jane, mumbling, "You're more trouble than you're worth," as he reached for her.

That red-tipped white cane shot out and whacked the robber's right hand. *Whap!* Immediately followed with

*Kapow!* as the semi-automatic went off and clattered to the floor. It landed on the wad of paper towels Betty Jo had left there. I knew what was under that pile, but I grabbed the gun anyway and aimed it at the robber, who was rubbing his hand where Jane had hit it with the cane.

"A girl won't shoot me," the robber said.

"I'm not a girl," I said. "I'm a *woman!*"

"And she's already shot one man," Jane added.

"Eeeeeeeeeeeeeh!" Betty Jo howled again and began shaking, working herself into a fresh hissy fit. "I knew y'all were crazy!" she cried.

"Call 911," I said and pointed to the wall phone behind the register.


The law men arrived and handcuffed the robber. "She's got a gun," he told the deputy.

"Yeah," I said. "I had yours, but they've got it now," and motioned toward the other officers.

Betty Jo had finally calmed down. We exchanged a look, and she vowed she'd never seen any gun except the robber's, which was technically the truth.

"She told me those two had a gun, too," the robber insisted.

Betty Jo and I just shook our heads in puzzled amazement.

By the time we'd each given a statement and signed it, Betty Jo's boss had arrived. He was happy to learn that nothing was missing. It was almost ten o'clock, but he assured me we were only about fifteen minutes from Planet Friendly Funeral Supplies. He even let me use the store phone to call Mr. Harper, who agreed to be waiting at his business for us and repeated directions to me several times.

The store owner insisted on treating us to large

coffees to go, compliments of the store.

As Jane and I started out the door, she turned around and told him, "You should be ashamed letting this young girl work here alone at night." He scowled. I rushed Jane to the hearse before she volunteered any more advice.

# Chapter Six

"I'd begun to worry about you," Al Harper said as he led Jane and me into his showroom, which was a very large metal building. He was a chubby fellow, balding on top with a long, curly brown ponytail hanging down his back. Probably in his mid-thirties.

We were in the largest casket showroom I'd ever seen. Harper guided us through a maze of woven coffins from extremely tiny, smaller than for a full term newborn baby to gigantic, big enough for a circus fat lady (or man, for that matter.) They were made of willow, wicker, rattan, cardboard and unusual materials I couldn't identify. I wondered if he had any made of sweet grass—the stuff my Gullah friend Rizzie weaves into baskets.

I was glad Jane couldn't see. No, I don't mean that at all. If there were anything I could do to make Jane see, I'd do it, including giving her one of my eyes if it would work. What I meant was that being there with coffins all around would have freaked her out if she could see them. Jane clenched my hand tightly as we followed Harper to a very attractive light golden brown woven coffin. I knew from the strength of her grip that the thought of being sur-rounded by caskets upset her even without seeing them.

"This is the one you want," he continued. "It's lined with environmentally friendly biodegradable leak-resistant sheeting, and a cardboard barrier beneath the lining protects the sheeting from being pierced by the wicker or willow." He sounded rehearsed, like a commercial.

Harper lifted the lid from the top and showed us the inside. "The unbleached lining, shroud, and pillow are all included in the price." He paused. "You did bring payment, didn't you?"

I took Odell's Middleton's Mortuary check from my purse and handed it to him.

He examined it carefully. Like I'd forge a check to buy a casket! "Well," he finally said, "if you'll go out and back your hearse up to the double doors, we'll get this baby loaded for you."

Jane stayed inside the building. She held her arms tight by her sides as though she were afraid she might accidentally touch a coffin. I backed the funeral coach to the open doors and pressed the button to release the funeral coach's rear entry locks. I left the engine running with the air conditioning on to cool off the interior before we started the long ride home. I jumped out, slammed my door closed, and went back into the building. Leaning over, I grabbed a wicker handle on the side of the casket we'd bought.

"No!" Mr. Harper shouted.

Jane jumped in response to his voice. "What's wrong?" she said.

"I'm sorry if I frightened you," he said to her, then turned to me. "We don't carry these by the handles. Use the shoulder carry and advise the funeral director to be sure the pall bearers don't attempt to move it by the handles."

"What do you mean carry it by the shoulders?" I asked. "Are you talking about where the body's shoulders will be?"

"I'm sure you've seen it in movies if not while working. Shoulder carry is used frequently during military funerals," Harper answered. "I've installed a plywood base in the bottom, so the weight of the body won't go through the wicker, but the whole bottom, including the base, could fall out if you move it by the handles. The shoulder carry is when a coffin is hoisted to the pall bearers' shoulders, spreading the weight."

*Then why'd they put handles on it?* That question stayed in my head and never escaped my lips.

Together, Mr. Harper and I carried the basket casket on our shoulders and slid it into the funeral coach. I closed and locked the rear doors. When I guided Jane to the passenger side and tried to open it for her, the lock wouldn't release. "Wait here," I said and walked around to the driver's side—my side.

I'd thought this trip couldn't get any worse, but it did. I'd set the locks on the doors. The casket was inside; Jane and I were outside; and the only key I had was in the ignition. My cell phone was on the seat. Mr. Harper had closed the double doors and walked to his van when I realized my problem.

"Is something wrong?" Harper called.

"I locked my keys inside," I answered.

He walked over and peered through the front glass.

"It's running," he said. *Duh? Like Jane and I were both too dense to notice.*

"That's where the keys are," I said.

Harper looked at his watch and grimaced, but he said, "Let me see if I have anything that will help. He went to the van and came back with a slender piece of metal, what Daddy calls a slim jim. Harper tried to slide it into the hearse, but the windows were too tight.

"I'm afraid you're going to need a locksmith unless someone can bring you a spare key." I figured that a locksmith probably wouldn't cost more than ten hours' labor for a part-time employee. Besides, if we waited here over five hours while Odell contacted someone and they drove up, it would be ten more hours instead of five before we got the casket to the funeral home.

"Do you have a number for a local locksmith, and may I use your phone to call him?"

"I'll call Lock Doc for you." He took a cell phone from his pocket and hit auto dial. It seemed a little strange to me for him to have their number programmed in, but maybe lots of people lock their keys inside the vehicle when they pick up caskets.

Jane and I stood by the funeral coach, waiting. My cell phone was ringing on the front seat. I could hear it through the windows and see it flashing. That's when I remembered Odell had told me to call him when I had the casket. He'd estimated our arrival as around eight that night, but after the fiasco when we stopped for coffee, I'd forgotten to call. It was now after eleven.

"May I use your phone?" I asked Harper.

He handed it to me and walked around nervously as I dialed the mortuary phone number. Unless someone had called with a pickup, Odell would have transferred the call to his cell phone by now.

"Hello," Odell growled.

"We're running behind," I said. "Can I just park at my place and bring the hearse and casket in tomorrow morning?"

"That's okay. I'm at the ER with Otis. I think the doctor's going to admit him." I could tell he was upset because he didn't scold me about calling the funeral coach a hearse.

"I thought Otis just had a cold or flu."

"His temperature shot up and he started having trouble breathing. I don't know what's going on, but you drive safely, and I'll see you in the morning. Be to work by eight if you can."

I disconnected. I hadn't told Odell about the keys because he'd sounded so distressed about Otis. They fuss at each other a lot, but they're identical twins who don't look alike anymore. When they started to lose their hair, Otis got plugs; Odell shaved his head. Odell is also a barbecue addict while Otis is a vegetarian who spends a lot of time in his tanning bed. I don't tell anyone, but the tanning bed is in the prep room at the funeral home. Odell wouldn't be caught dead in it. I've been tempted to try it, but I haven't yet.

In any event, though they look very different now, they still have that twin thing going and relate to each other far more than my brothers.

The Lock Doc arrived. A bald-headed guy with a picture of himself painted on the side of his van, wearing the same clothes he had on—green scrubs with "Doc" embroidered on the shirt. It only took him a few seconds to open the driver's side of the hearse. I pushed the necessary buttons to unlock Jane's side and walked her around. When I closed the door behind her, I moved to the driver's side and pulled out the Middleton's Visa card. That's when the Lock Doc told me he only accepted cash. He called himself "Doc," but from the price he quoted, you'd have thought he was a brain surgeon.

"I'm sorry, I don't have that much cash with me," I said.

Mr. Harper had been pacing back and forth since we discovered the keys were locked inside the funeral coach. He kept looking at his watch. When Doc turned his attention to Mr. Harper and began scolding him for calling and authorizing the work if I didn't have cash to pay for it, Harper offered to run the Visa card through his machine and pay the locksmith cash. With that last bit of business completed, Jane and I headed for home.

Jane hadn't been company on the way to Tanner, and

she wasn't on the way back to St. Mary either. She was snoring before we reached the South Carolina state line, and she didn't stop until we pulled into our driveway in St. Mary at almost five in the morning.

# Chapter Seven

"Callie Parrish, I need to talk to you *right now!*" Sheriff Harmon shouted over the instrumental version of "Just As I Am" announcing he'd opened the front door. He sounded upset, and I'd already had enough of upset men for today. With only three hours' sleep, I'd arrived at Middleton's at nine A.M. Odell had been pacing when I arrived. He was in a hurry to go to the hospital and check on Otis and irritated with me for making him late.

Stepping out of my office, I pulled the door closed behind me and walked toward the foyer. "I'm here," I called, though not so loud as Harmon had yelled for me. The Middleton twins had trained me never to raise my voice in the funeral home.

"Where did you get that set of fingerprints that were on the table when I was here yesterday?" He pulled them from his pocket. *No wonder I hadn't found them!*

"I took them from Mr. Joyner. His wife brought in a brochure about a business called Print Memories. According to the pamphlet, the bereaved can have their mortuary take the loved one's fingerprints. The company makes memorial silver and gold pendants, cufflinks, and other jewelry with the prints on them."

"So these prints really *are* from a corpse here at the funeral home?" Harmon asked, waving my missing set of cards at me.

"I've been looking all over for those. How'd you get them?"

The sheriff ignored my question.

"Show me the corpse these prints came from," he demanded.

"Follow me," I said and headed toward the cooler.

When I pulled Mr. Joyner from his drawer, he looked as good as he did when we'd brought him in. He still lay in his navy blue pajamas, and there wasn't yet any sign of discoloration or skin slippage.

"And you're sure those fingerprints came from him?" the sheriff asked.

"Yeah, I took them myself." I paused.

"Did you know the Joyner family before the body was picked up?" Harmon asked.

"No, they're from Hilton Head. Why? Can I have the prints back?"

The sheriff ignored my question and said, "I accidentally took the cards with me. When I realized it, I put them on my desk so I'd be sure to bring them back. Do you print all bodies?"

"Oh, no. These were just because the widow wants a gold and diamond charm bracelet with his prints on the charms. I'm sure glad you've got the cards, so I don't have to do them over."

"Tell you what, Callie. I'll make a new set and give you back your original ones. I need a chain of evidence that the prints I turn in came from this corpse." Sheriff Harmon pointed at Mr. Joyner and removed a plastic bag with cards and ink pad from his coat pocket.

"What are you talking about, chain of evidence? Odell said Mr. Joyner had an attack of gastroenteritis while he was in Beaufort. Went in the hospital there for a few days, then died. He wasn't murdered or anything like that."

"In this case, Callie, the corpse wasn't a homicide

victim. He's a *killer.*" The sheriff began rolling fingerprints as he talked. Like Odell had suggested after I'd taken the first set of prints, Harmon inked the finger, then rolled the paper against it instead of rolling the finger against the paper.

"That new deputy, Eddie Blake, is the most eager beaver I've ever had working for me. Some of the fellows have started calling him Fast Eddie. He saw the print cards and put them through AFIS without even talking to me about it. I was ticked off until the results came back," Harmon said.

"AFIS as in Automated Fingerprint Identification System?" I asked. I'd read about the computerized operation.

"Un-hunh. AFIS got a hit on them. Your Mr. Joyner is Johnny Johnson, a missing person, alleged killer during the Buckley armored car robbery in 1980. He was one of the FBI's most wanted until terrorists and more vicious killers claimed all the top spots."

"Johnny Johnson?" I asked and rolled my eyes—just a little.

"Don't laugh. I once arrested a Tommy Thompson. When is Johnson's funeral scheduled?"

"This afternoon."

"No way!"

"Well, you can't hold him too long. His wife doesn't want him embalmed."

"I need contact information for Mrs. Johnson."

"She's not Mrs. Johnson. She goes by the name 'Mrs. Joyner' even though they weren't legally married. I can give you the home number and one for her cell as well as their address."

"I need to run these new prints I made through AFIS. If the report's the same, I'll have to notify New Jersey and the FBI."

"Come on to the office and I'll give you the info for Mrs. Joyner." As we went down the hall, I said, "I think I remember reading about that robbery. It was in New York, right?"

"You're probably thinking about the Brinks robbery. That's completely different." Harmon held the door for me to enter the office. I may be a modern young lady, but I still like those courtesies. "Brinks was the name of the armored car company. That happened in New York state a year or so after the Buckley robbery."

The Joyner folder lay on my desk. I copied Grace's phone numbers and address onto a Post-It for the sheriff. He pulled his little notebook from his pocket and transferred the information to it. "I can't keep up with those tiny scraps of paper," he complained.

*Well, ex-cuuze me!* I thought it but didn't say it. One time the sheriff told me that if he ever heard me say "excuse me" or "whatever" again, he'd spank me. Of course, he was over at the house eating my dad's catfish stew when he said it, so I don't think it was official.

"What about this Johnny Johnson?" I asked.

"I gotta go," he said.

Following him to the front door, I bombarded him with more questions. He stopped and said, "Three men robbed an armored car at a mall in Buckley, New Jersey, so Buckley refers to the location, not the armored car company. They didn't go in blasting like the Brinks robbery, but before it was over, a guard was taken from the scene and later shot dead. The police captured one of the robbers, but the other two got away with several million dollars, which was way more in the early eighties than it is now."

"Was Johnny Johnson caught or did he get away?"

"They captured Leon McDonald, but he was killed by another prisoner before he even went to trial. Johnson and the other suspect, Noah Gordon, disappeared along with the money. I'm thinking Johnny Johnson moved down here and started over with a new name, and from what you're saying, a new wife. He left his second wife and three kids in New Jersey."

"I've never heard about that case," I said.

"It was pretty big news at the time, but the Brinks robbery was so much bigger that almost anytime an armored car robbery is mentioned, people think of it. Of course, here in South Carolina, we think of the armored car heist in Richland County in 2007. Those guys got almost ten million dollars."

"I remember," I said.

Harmon was pulling the door closed behind him when he said, "Don't let them bury that body until I tell you it's okay."

"Well, if you're going to talk to Mrs. Joyner, *you* tell her we can't bury her husband. She's already bought the tree. She delivered it yesterday while I'd gone to pick up the casket. It's in a big pot on the loading dock."

"Tree?"

"She's planting a crape myrtle in his memory as part of the ceremony."

"Keep that corpse right where it is until I'm back." He closed the door, and I returned to my office. I'd looked up "armored car robberies" on the Internet before he was out of our parking lot. Apparently, they weren't as rare as I'd thought because there were tons of entries. Well, not a ton, but a lot of them on the screen. Sure enough, there were more entries about the Brinks heist on October 20, 1981, in Nanuet, New York, than any other.

"Just a Closer Walk with Thee" tore me away from the computer just as I'd gotten the price for Mrs. Joyner's bracelet. Mrs. Joyner stood in the front hall with a dry-cleaner bag over one arm and a bouquet of wild flowers tied with raffia in her other hand.

"I want these on top of the casket," she said and handed me the flowers. "Did you see the tree?" she asked.

"Odell told me about it and I took a look. It's beautiful!" She followed me to the kitchen where I put the flowers into a vase of water.

"It's a white crape myrtle. I thought that would be a good choice because they grow well here, but they're not wild. There are some really pretty pinks, but I think white's better for a man." She wiped a tear from her eye. "I've brought clothes for Harry to be buried in. I don't believe in displaying dead people, but I don't want him laid to rest in pajamas either." She handed me the hanger.

"I'll dress him," I said.

"You'll dress him? Harry was kind of modest. I think he'd prefer a man to change his clothes."

"Dressing the deceased is my job, but I'm sure Odell will be happy to take care of it." I cleared my throat. "By the way, Sheriff Harmon wants to talk to you. Do you have your cell phone with you?"

"Right here," she said and held up an iPhone.

"Arms of an Angel" played loudly. The sound startled her, but she flipped the phone open and answered, "Hello."

*Shameless.* Garth Brooks used to sing about that, and it's the best word to describe my standing there eavesdropping. I knew I should take the clothes she'd brought and step away to give her some privacy. I knew it, but . . . I didn't do it.

"Yes, this is Grace Joyner. Who'd you say you are? . . . Well, you see my husband died, and the funeral is this afternoon. Couldn't I talk to you in a few days when all of this is over? . . . You'll come *here* to the mortuary to speak to me? If you insist, then I'll wait." She closed the phone.

Grace Joyner's expression was complete confusion.

"That was the sheriff. Like you said, he wants to talk to me. Says he's coming over here."

"Yes, ma'am. Would you like to sit in the conference room while you wait?"

"What I'd really like to do is see my husband."

I don't know exactly how long refrigeration delays decomposition, but there'd been no signs of deterioration when Sheriff Harmon and I looked at Mr. Joyner only a short while earlier. I assumed it would be all right with Odell for her to see him.

"There's been no body preparation," I said.

"Not supposed to be," she said.

I led the way to the cooler. She bit her lip when I pulled out Mr. Joyner's tray and unzipped the body bag off his face. I knew it wasn't the first time she'd seen him dead because Jake had told me Mrs. Joyner was still in the hospital room when he went for the pickup. A few more silent tears trickled down her cheeks as she moved closer and reached out her hand. I tensed, ready to stop her if she went berserk and grabbed the body.

Buh-leeve me. We'd had loved ones try to climb into the casket with the deceased. There's no telling what she might have tried. No problem. She stroked the side of his face several times, turned her back, and walked out. I zipped the bag and slid the body back in the cooler before I joined her in the hall.

"Let's go to the conference room," I suggested. "Would you like a cup of coffee or tea while we wait on the sheriff?"

"Yes, coffee would be nice."

I left her sitting in a big green overstuffed chair while I made coffee. She looked even smaller in such a large seat. Knowing Sheriff Harmon would want some, I set out three Wedgwood cups and saucers along with the coffee service. I placed the silver tray on the conference table just as "Blessed Assurance" played. I stuck my head into the hall and motioned to Sheriff Harmon.

He joined us and put a small recorder on the table beside the coffee service, pushed the button, and went into official law enforcement mode.

"Mrs. Joyner, I'm Wayne Harmon, Sheriff of Jade County. Do you agree to talk to me of your own free will?"

"Of course, but are you arresting me for something?"

"No, ma'am. I'm not arresting you."

"Then why the Miranda?" she asked.

"I'm not reading you the Miranda. Some questions have come up about your husband, and I'm hoping you can help answer them. I just like to have agreement on tape anytime I record questioning."

"I'll tell you anything you want, but I have to warn you that Harry was almost paranoid about keeping his business private. I may not know everything you ask."

"Mrs. Joyner, did Harry ever go by another name?"

"Not that I know of. I met him when I was waiting tables at the golf club. He introduced himself as Harold Joyner."

"Middle name?"

"Harold was the middle name. His first name was John."

"John Harold Joyner?"

"That's right."

"When did you marry him?"

"Legally, we're not married unless it's by those South Carolina Common Law rules, which I've heard have been changed. He gave me these rings on a cruise, but we never made it legal." She waggled her left hand at him to be sure he saw those multi-karat diamonds.

"I understand the services are scheduled for this afternoon," Harmon continued.

"That's right. I don't believe in all the pomp and circumstance and displaying dead people. Harry will have an eco-friendly graveside burial with just a few friends I've invited. Then we're planting a tree in his memory."

I'm not proud of what crossed my mind. *Would they plant the tree above his head like a grave marker or in the middle of the plot?* I shook my head slightly. Like that would clear away the unwanted visions of trees growing out of Mr. Joyner's various body parts. I remembered an old movie and several short stories where killers planted flowers over their victims in the back yard.

"I'm going to be totally upfront with you," the sheriff said to Mrs. Joyner. "We have reason to believe that Harry Joyner may be a long missing man named Johnny Johnson. Did he ever mention that name to you?"

"No."

"Did Mr. Joyner work?"

"I assumed he'd retired before I met him. We traveled a lot, mainly in the continental United States and on short cruises. Come to think of it, we never went anywhere that required a passport. I'd been married four times before Harry and I got together. I was happy with him. He always paid the bills, and he gave me a very liberal monthly allowance."

"If you don't have access to his funds, how will you pay for his services?" the sheriff asked.

"And what about his hospital bill?" I interrupted before Mrs. Joyner could answer. Every time I go to the hospital, they want my insurance card before they treat me. The sheriff glared at me—a look that made me realize he'd forgotten I was there and that I should've kept my mouth shut.

"We paid a large cash deposit when Harry went into the hospital. I paid the balance before I left when he died. I don't have any insurance papers or his social security number, but I do have funds to pay for his services." She gave me a reassuring look.

"What about his driver's license?" Sheriff Harmon asked.

"He didn't have one. He didn't like to drive. When I met him, he traveled by cab. After we got together, I was always our chauffeur when we went anywhere."

"Mrs. Joyner, it sounds as though your husband probably is Johnny Johnson. I'm afraid you're going to have to postpone his funeral."

The little woman bristled. "I've already called people and invited them—our friends from the club as well as Harry's golfing buddies." She almost spat out the words.

"I have no intention of changing the burial plans. You can't arrest him. He's *dead.*"

"No, I can't arrest him, but Callie told me you're not having him embalmed. I'm glad of that."

"Why?"

"Because if the FBI wants to examine the body, it needs to be refrigerated until they arrive, but not embalmed. They'll probably want an autopsy, and it's best to do that before embalming. I've contacted them, and I understand they're sending a couple of agents down."

"I'm telling you they'd better get here fast, because I'm burying Harry this afternoon."

"Mrs. Joyner, if you won't cooperate, I'll have to take legal steps."

"I don't see what legal moves you can make. You can't arrest me. I've done nothing wrong. You can't arrest Harry. He's dead."

"I'll be back shortly," Harmon said, turned on his heel, and left.

Grace Joyner said. "Just proceed with everything. You got the casket, didn't you?"

"Yes, ma'am. Would you like to see it?"

The wicker coffin was sitting on a bier in my workroom. I led her to it, and she exclaimed with joy that it was, "Perfect. Absolutely perfect!"

That woman inspected the basket casket like it was a piece of fine furniture she was buying. She ran her hands over the outside and the inside. She liked the fact it had a pillow, which I thought was kind of strange. To me, the purpose of a pillow in a casket was to help me position the deceased's head properly. Most bereaved people seem to think it looks more comfortable. But why would a pillow be important if she didn't want anyone to see him? If all she wanted was for the body to decompose as rapidly as possible?

Mrs. Joyner lifted the casket by the side and peeked under it. There were two small wooden runners attached to the bottom. "What are those for?" she asked.

"They were already installed when I picked the coffin up," I said. "The supplier said their purpose is to help the casket slide easily into the crematorium. I know you aren't planning on cremation, but we left them on."

"Oh," she said. Her eyes darted around nervously. "I'm going now," she said. "I'll be back at one o'clock. Please have Harry dressed in the clothes I brought. He's not to be shown to any of the guests, but I'd like to see him one more time before you seal the casket to carry it to the resting place."

*Seal* the casket? There's no seal on a woven casket. It looked to me like there were several little rattan straps that looped together when it was closed, but it certainly didn't seal.

Personally, I have to fight back a smile every time anyone mentions sealing a casket anyway. What people consider *sealed* does keep out moisture and insects for a while, but no casket seals totally airtight. Decomposition produces gases that would blow the container to pieces if provisions weren't made for them to escape. Otis had explained that to me right after I came to work at Middleton's.

With nothing else needing to be done, I went back and set out the clothes for Mr. Joyner. I'd expected the garment bag to hold a suit, but these were Hilton Head retirees. Grace Joyner had brought him an expensive pair of khakis and a green golf shirt with Hilton Head Dunes embroidered over the chest pocket. The shirt was like the one worn by the dead man in the Jaguar with the snake. I wondered if they had ever golfed together.

# Chapter Eight

Dark bags under his eyes and worry lines on his forehead. Odell came in through the rear employees' door, so no music announced his arrival. He looked worse than I'd ever seen him. I hesitated, but then asked, "How's Otis?"

"Not good. Not good at all. I thought pneumonia was easy to cure these days, but the doctor says Otis is touch and go. He didn't respond to the first meds they tried.

"Now they've changed the antibiotic and got him on IV's as well as oxygen."

"I'm so sorry, Odell. If you want to stay at the hospital, I'll call in some of the part-timers. We can handle the Joyner service without you or Otis." I paused, then added, "That is, if the sheriff lets us have it."

"I might take you up on that." His whole demeanor turned melancholy. "You know Otis was always the healthier twin," he continued. "Maybe because of the difference in our life styles. It just doesn't seem real to see Doofus lying up there looking so sick in that hospital bed. That doctor friend of yours came by. Said someone in the ER told him Otis was there. He said to tell you hello and that he's not the primary physician for Otis, but he'll check on him."

"He'll do it, too. Dr. Don's a womanizer, but he's a good doctor."

"Now, Callie. There's a little bit of dawg in a lotta

men, but if I remember correctly, you only dated him a few times. That's not really enough to expect commitment."

This was a discussion I didn't want to have, so I told Odell that Mrs. Joyner wanted him to dress her husband instead of me. After Odell had the body clothed, I began putting Mr. Joyner's socks on him. Sure enough, his wife had brought tennis shoes. No golf shoes with non-biodegradable spikes. Probably the only reason she wasn't burying him with a golf club was because it wouldn't decay back to the earth.

When we'd finished, Odell slid Mr. Joyner back into his drawer and then wheeled the bier with the basket casket into the area right outside the cooling slots. We'd casket him right before the service.

Odell said, "I'm going by and pick up some things Otis needs from his place. I'll take them to the hospital and either call you or come back by time for lunch." I've never seen him as dejected as he appeared as he left.

The phone rang. I answered, for some reason expecting it to be Mrs. Joyner, but the caller was Molly, my brother Bill's fiancée.

"I just talked to the lady at the Beautiful Brides Boutique, and she says you're the only one of my attendants who hasn't been by to have her dress fitted. When are you going?" Molly sounded distressed and fussy. "Will you please go over there at lunch time?"

"Things are kinda tight here. Otis is in the hospital and we have an early afternoon funeral. I'll go tomorrow."

"Please don't forget." I heard tears in her voice. So far both of the soon-to-be-brides engaged to my brothers had called and cried at me. Maybe finding the "right" man wasn't all it's cracked up to be.

"I'll go tomorrow, I promise. Is there anything else I can do for you?"

"Yes, there is. I want to know if you know *why* your brother bought a *purple* truck right before our wedding. That's going to look awful in the going away photos. First, he does that, then all of a sudden he says Jane wants her and Frank to have a double wedding with Bill and me. The wedding is almost here. Do you have any idea what's going on?"

"I knew he was planning to buy a new truck, but I didn't know it was purple. You could rent a fancy car for the pictures when you leave the reception. Depending on how busy we are, Bill could even talk to Odell and see if he could borrow a vehicle from Middleton's for that night."

"I'm not using a hearse at my wedding!!"

"I didn't mean a hearse, but if you don't want anything from the funeral home, you can borrow my Mustang. That would be sporty."

"Not going to ride off in an *old* Mustang either!"

Ex-cuuze me. It's a *vintage* car, but I didn't have time to discuss that with her. "From what I heard about it, that double wedding business isn't Jane's idea." I said. "Why don't you just say 'no' and have it over with? That way you and Jane will both be happy."

"I can't believe that! Bill and Frank have been telling me it was Jane's idea and that she really wants your two brothers to have a double wedding."

"Maybe the four of you should sit down together and talk it over."

"Good idea, and please get the final fitting on your dress. You know the wedding is almost here."

"Yes, I know. I'll go tomorrow, for sure."

"And don't forget the couples shower my aunts are giving Saturday. You can bring a date if you want."

*Yeah, like which of my numerous suitors would I want to take to a shower where my daddy and four of my brothers will be present?*

"Jane and Frank will be there. Maybe I could ask them to come early and we could talk."

"No, Molly, I think you should handle this today. Why not call now and ask the three of them over this evening?"

"You're probably right. By the way, how's your dog?" Big Boy had been a gift from Molly through my brother, her fiancé Bill.

"He's fine, still growing though. The vet says he's one of the largest Great Danes she's ever seen."

"Terrific! I'll see you Saturday then." I could probably have said Big Boy had turned purple with yellow spots and could sing "The Star Spangled Banner," and Molly would have responded the same way. I didn't think my answer really mattered to her.


"Miss Parrish! Miss Parrish!" The voice was louder than "The Old Rugged Cross."

I left my desk and headed for the front door. The new deputy I'd seen at the bookstore yesterday was running down the hall, yelling my name.

"May I help you?" I said.

"You're Callie Parrish?"

"That's right."

"Sheriff Harmon sent me to tell you not to move Johnny Johnson's body from the Frigidaire before he gets here. He's on the way with a warrant." The man talked faster than I could think.

"First, it's not a refrigerator. Second, what kind of warrant? He can't arrest a dead man."

"I'm Eddie Blake, new to Jade County Sheriff's Department, and I understood that I was to guard the corpse until the sheriff arrives. I'd appreciate your leading me to it."

"There's no need to watch Mr. Joyner. He's in a slot in the cooler. No one's here but me, and I'm not planning to pull him out."

"What's a slot?"

"It's like a drawer."

Blake stood up taller and straighter. He also raised his voice at me. "Ma'am, I *demand* access to that corpse so that I can do my duty."

The back door closed, and I knew that Odell had returned. It only took a minute for him to reach us. "What do you mean screaming in a funeral home? Have you no respect?" Odell growled.

"Just following orders. Who are you?" Blake said.

"I'm Odell Middleton, one of the proprietors of this establishment, and you met me when I picked up the man found in the Jaguar over at Best Books yesterday. You run around trying to look so efficient yet you don't remember anybody. Part of law enforcement in small towns is knowing the citizens. Wayne Harmon told me you'd come highly recommended by the Philadelphia Police Department, but you got a way to go to be successful in St. Mary."

Blake had the good grace to look embarrassed, but when Sheriff Harmon came in, the deputy immediately began complaining.

"I told them you wanted me to guard the body, but they won't let me," he whined.

"I didn't tell you to *guard* the corpse. I told you to let them know I was on the way with what we need to postpone the funeral."

"And what do you have?" Odell grumbled.

"Since Mrs. Joyner is so adamant she wouldn't put off the service until the FBI arrives, I got a subpoena from Judge Cain."

"You got an arrest warrant for a dead man?" Puh-leese. I knew I should be quiet, but I couldn't control my mouth.

"No, Callie," Harmon sighed. "Of course I'm not going to arrest a corpse. I've got a subpoena for Mr. Joyner or Mr. Johnson, as I believe he really is, as evidence. Not a witness, not a suspect. Just as evidence. And not indefinitely. Judge Cain gave me seventy-two hours, but the FBI agent should be here late this afternoon."

"I didn't know you could do that!" Blake's face lit up like a kid on Christmas morning.

Odell glared at the deputy. "There's a lot you don't know," he said before he turned to Harmon. "Have you notified Mrs. Joyner that we can't bury her husband today? I had the tent and chairs set up this morning, and the grave has been dug."

"She was here when I told Callie the funeral would have to be postponed, but she didn't believe I could do that. Maybe I should have Blake stay until she's seen the warrant."

*Just what we need. Blake here to handle a distraught, but strong-willed, widow.*

My thoughts were needless. The front door opened. "Just As I Am" sounded, and Grace Joyner entered. Her eyes darted from me to Blake to Odell to Harmon, then back to me.

"What's going on?" she asked.

"Mrs. Joyner, the sheriff has obtained legal permission from Judge Cain to require a seventy-two-hour postpone- ment of Mr. Joyner's burial," Odell said in a voice almost as Undertaking 101 as Otis usually sounded. "Of course," he continued, "you may have a service here today and then have interment in a few days if you like."

"You know I don't want that. Just a few friends at graveside." She glared at Harmon. "Tell me the truth. Is there anything I can do to keep you from stopping me burying my husband today?"

"No, ma'am." Harmon cleared his throat. "And believe me, I wouldn't have taken this action if I didn't feel it's absolutely necessary."

Grace Joyner's whole demeanor changed. "If there's nothing I can do, I'll just have to regroup," she said softly. "I doubt I can contact everyone I invited in time to stop them going to Taylor's. Can I just have a little commemorative service and plant the tree today? Actually burying the body isn't as important to me as planting the memorial tree."

"Of course," Odell answered.

"And I don't want any big funeral home vehicles," Mrs. Joyner said. "I'll carry the tree to Taylor's Cemetery in my car. It's really not necessary for any of you to go."

"Mrs. Joyner, one of us will accompany you. We don't have to use anything you consider a gas-guzzler. I've made arrangements for some more fuel efficient cars to use today."

"Cancel them," Mrs. Joyner ordered. "I'll let Callie ride with me, and I'll bring her back after it's over."


By noon, I was in Mrs. Joyner's hybrid. She was driving, and the crape myrtle tree was sticking out the back with a red flag blowing in the breeze. Mrs. Joyner was lecturing me on crape myrtles. At least I was getting paid to listen. When Daddy or Otis go into teaching/preaching mode, I have to hear it off the clock.

"The reason I chose a crape myrtle is because it's an ornamental that can be controlled by pruning. Besides, Harry loved flowers, and I think the white blossoms are so pretty." She continued with a lot of facts about proper pruning to make the plant a tree rather than all bushy.

I tuned her out and wondered how Otis was doing.

Odell had gone back to the hospital. He'd called in Denise Sharpe to answer the telephone. We'd been using her as a part-time receptionist since her previous employer, Nate's Sports and Subs, closed. Just as the Middletons required me to wear black dresses, Denise had to wear them, too. Hers, however, had to have long sleeves and turtleneck collars to hide her piercings and tattoos.

Taylor's Cemetery is a very old graveyard about an hour from St. Mary. It's not a perpetual care graveyard, so people maintain their loved ones' plots. Some were carefully manicured grass or covered with white pebbles. Others were overgrown with weeds. The markers stood in all sizes from one foot tall to fourteen feet angels. The front of the acreage faced a country road. The other three sides were bordered by thick trees.

I'd been there several times on behalf of Middleton's. The most memorable visit was the exhumation of a lady buried ten years previously. Her granddaughter won the state lottery and moved the old woman's grave to a perpetual care facility. For sure, I hadn't forgotten that day.

Odell had said he'd had the grave dug and an awning erected. The canvas covering wasn't one of ours. It had Clark's Funeral Services printed on the flap. Clark's was located closer to Taylor's Cemetery. Odell must have subbed out the work instead of rounding up some of our part-timers for the job.

Parked along the drive through the grounds were cars that wouldn't have passed Mrs. Joyner's "no gas-guzzlers" criteria. The majority of them were Cadillacs, Mercedes, and beemers. Even one Hummer. Mrs. Joyner's choice of proper burial attire for her husband might be golfing clothes, but the attendees had dressed in traditional, appropriate funeral attire—suits for the men, dark garments and heels for the ladies. They stood respectfully around the tent, waiting for the widow before sitting in the folding chairs.

Mrs. Joyner nudged me and whispered, "Stay with me." I followed her to the front row. It only took a second for me to realize exactly where the tent and open grave were. Taylor's Cemetery had sold Mrs. Joyner the same space we'd invaded to disinter the grandmother. I wondered if Mrs. Joyner had gotten a discounted price or if she even knew she'd bought her husband a used cemetery plot.

A man who may or may not have been a minister stood. I couldn't really tell because he wore a light blue suit but no clerical collar, cross, or anything like that. I can spot Catholic and Episcopal priests as well as Lutheran pastors, by how they dress. It's impossible to distinguish other denominations by looks. Have to wait 'til they start preaching.

After Mrs. Joyner and I sat, people crowded under the tent and were seated behind us. A few bouquets of fresh flowers lay around the grave, which was covered by green Astroturf and roped off. A hole for the tree was dug at the head of the site.

I'd noticed that no floral arrangements had been delivered to the mortuary even though Mrs. Joyner hadn't had us mention a charity for donations "in lieu of flowers" in the obituary. She'd also had the services posted as "private, by invitation only." Apparently, she'd told the privileged guests that she favored natural bunches of flowers over professionally assembled wreaths and sprays. I didn't know if this was typical of ecologically friendly funerals or simply the widow's preference.

The gentleman in charge opened with a prayer. The main topic was preservation of the earth and its resources. That's what he talked about when he began the eulogy, too. Realizing that the absence of clerical robes and collar meant we wouldn't be jumping up and down throughout most of the service, I let my mind drift. I was thinking about my brothers' upcoming weddings when I noticed a bright purple truck shining through the trees at the back of the cemetery. I barely heard the engine cranking before I watched a purple Ford 350 dually pull out of the trees and exit in the opposite direction from the cars at Mr. Joyner's site.

My heart thudded in my chest. I wanted to scream. I wanted to chase that truck. To stop it and demand, "Bill, what in the name of heaven are you doing parked in the back of a cemetery with some woman who is not the one you're marrying?"

I couldn't do any of the above.

The truck sped out of the gate and up the road. By the time my thoughts returned to the present, Mrs. Joyner was holding the crape myrtle tree upright in the hole while mourners walked past and dropped clumps of dirt around the tree like the "dust to dust" casting of soil onto a casket as part of a regular service. After that, each of them came by again and sprinkled water from a fancy container. The service concluded, and Mrs. Joyner spent the next thirty minutes talking with her guests.

I was so mad at Bill that I could hardly bear waiting for Mrs. Joyner to take me back to St. Mary. When most everyone else had gone, she finally told me she was ready to go. I climbed in and rode in silence for a while. "Are you okay?" she asked after about thirty minutes.

"I'm all right," I said. "How are you?"

"I'm as fine as I can be under the circumstances. I thought the service went well, didn't you?"

"It was beautiful," I answered though I really had no opinion at all. When my thoughts finally got off my brother Bill and back to the tree-planting, I wondered again if the widow knew they'd sold her a used plot. I wanted to ask her, but I felt that Otis and Odell wouldn't be pleased if I said anything about it.

# Chapter Nine

Otis and Odell's niece. That's who I became when I arrived at the hospital patient information desk and asked for Otis Middleton's room number.

"He's been moved into Medical Intensive Care and can only be seen by two family members for ten minutes every two hours. Are you a relative?" the clerk asked.

"Yes," I lied, feeling guilty, but justified. "I'm his niece."

"Oh, you must be his brother's child," she said. Like Magdalena, Tamar Myers's character in her Pennsylvania Dutch mysteries, the clerk must have gotten her exercise by jumping to conclusions. "I think your dad is in the Coronary Intensive Care waiting area now," she continued. Like if I *were* Otis's niece, I'd have to be Odell's daughter. I could have been the child of another brother or a sister. Of course, they had no other siblings, but they *could* have.

"The orange steps lead to Intensive Care. Just follow them." Her words brought me back to reality and away from thinking of additional branches on the Middleton family tree.

I looked down and saw that the floor had different colored footprints painted on the tiles. I guess if you knew the color code, they would lead you just about anywhere in the hospital.

"Thanks," I mumbled and set out following the

orange outlines. I wondered where the yellow ones went. I'd always been a big fan of *The Wizard of Oz*, and fantasized about following the yellow brick road.

Those orange steps led into the elevator and out again with a big orange arrow by a number three painted on the wall. I got off on the third floor. At the end of the hall, I saw double doors with a sign that said, "Do NOT Enter. Intensive Care." I headed there to ask where the waiting room was, but Odell called my name before I got to the doors. I looked to the left and saw him sitting with other worried-looking people in a small room with lots of fake plants and a television showing some program about "Your Hospital Stay." No one paid any attention to it, and someone had turned the volume to "mute."

I joined the others and told Odell, "I'm scared to ask how he is. I didn't know he was in Intensive Care."

"It's not good right now. He isn't responding to treatment." Odell sat beside an older blonde-haired lady. She truly fit the description of a *yaller-haired* woman. Heavily made up, but not cheap-looking, she wore a pink dress with floral appliqués on the shoulder. In other words, she was wearing a painted-on corsage. The dress cinched in to her small waist, accenting a full bosom and robust hips. Her fingernails and toenails were painted a hot pink that picked up one of the tones in the flowers.

A gentleman sitting on the other side of Odell moved across the room. I thanked him and sat. Odell asked a few questions, and I assured him that the tree-planting had gone well and that Denise would forward any calls to my cell. She'd also promised to lock up at eight o'clock. The sheriff and the FBI agent hadn't arrived when Mrs. Joyner dropped me off at the funeral home. I didn't mention seeing Bill at Taylor's Cemetery, nor the fact he hadn't answered when I called him.

"Odell," I said, "Mrs. Joyner's hybrid vehicle was a

good ride. I thought you couldn't go but a few miles at a time in those cars. If the Mustang ever totally dies on me, I might get one."

"Not unless you get a different job," Odell said. "No way can we pay you the salary you'd need to buy one like hers. Folks who own them aren't trying to economize, just trying not to use up gasoline."

A woman wearing a hospital volunteer uniform stepped into the room. "It's six o'clock," she said. "Two members of each family may visit for ten minutes."

Odell turned toward the blonde. "Darlene," he said and motioned toward me, "this is Callie Parrish. She works at the funeral home. I've seen Otis every visiting time since they moved him to ICU, you and Callie go in now. I'll see Otis at eight."

Darlene leaned across Odell and said, "Thanks," to him, then, "Hello," to me. Her voice sounded really familiar, but I couldn't identify it. We followed the volunteer past several curtained-off spaces where others folks from the waiting room stopped and slipped in to see their relatives. The lady turned toward us and asked, "Are you here to see Mr. Middleton?"

"Yes," Darlene and I said in unison.

"Relationship?" she questioned.

I said, "Niece."

My mouth almost flew open when Darlene said, "Wife."

I'd never heard any mention of Otis being married. I knew Odell had two ex-wives, but nothing about Otis. He was a very private person and hadn't ever spoken of having been married. He didn't date, so I'd always assumed he wasn't interested in women.

The nurse held the beige curtain back for us. Otis lay motionless on a narrow hospital bed. His eyes were closed, and there were IV tubes and wires reaching from his body to several machines.

Darlene leaned over to him and patted his fingers below the needles in his arms and hands. "Otis?" she said softly. "Are you awake?"

He didn't open his eyes, but he muttered, "Darlene?"

"Yes, Big Boy," she said, and my mouth flew open for real this time. We'd both chosen the same pet name. Her choice for Otis was the same as mine for my dog.

After a few minutes, she stepped back and motioned for me to move up to Otis. I was so shocked at how bad he looked that I couldn't think of what to say.

"Just tell him who you are and that you're here," Darlene whispered. I'd been around Otis for several years now, and this woman had just surfaced after who knew how many years. I felt awkward that she seemed to be in charge. I wondered how long they'd been married and how long they'd been parted.

"Otis," I said and patted his hand as Darlene had. "It's Callie. I came to see how you're doing, but I don't want you to talk. Save all your strength to get well."

He didn't attempt to answer. Darlene and I stood silently until the nurse moved the curtain aside and said, "Time's up."

Back in the waiting room, Dr. Don Walters stood with Odell. "I've checked the charts, Otis may be showing a tiny bit of improvement," Don said. He grinned at me. "And what," he said, "is your relationship to Otis?"

"You've never heard me call him 'Uncle Otis'?" I said.

"No, but I won't tell on you." He turned toward Darlene. "Odell tells me you're Otis's wife," he said.

"Actually *ex-wife*, but I didn't know if that was a suitable kinship to get me back there to see him."

"Close enough," Don said. He turned toward Odell. "I'll come back around seven o'clock and check on him. Why don't you guys go have some coffee and sandwiches in the cafeteria?"

*Guys?* Don and I hadn't been on a date lately, but he'd never referred to me as a *guy* even when we quit going out. I straightened up and stuck my chest out before I realized that without the inflatable bra I used to wear, I didn't have any bosom.

Perhaps something showed in my eyes because he gave me a warmer look.

"Haven't seen you in a while, Callie. I'll give you a call. We can have dinner some night."

The doctor walked away before I answered him. Darlene smiled and said,

"It seems the good doctor would like to date you."

"Been there, done that," I quipped.

"They date off and on," Odell said.

A wicked look spread across Darlene's face. "Off and on or on and off? Sounds like fun to me."

"That's *not* how I meant it," Odell said.

"In Mae's words," Darlene giggled as she spoke, "'Don't keep a man guessing too long—he's sure to find the answer somewhere else.'"

"Don't start that kind of talk. Callie is a young lady," Odell growled.

"'It's hard to be funny when you have to be clean,'" Darlene teased.

"More Mae?" Odell asked.

"Yep, I've got hundreds of them."

We walked to the cafeteria (pink footprints). Odell was disappointed that they didn't have barbecue, and we all settled on club sandwiches. I've always liked the way club sandwiches come cut into triangles and stand up around chips on the plate.

I took a sip of coffee and told Darlene, "I didn't know Otis had been married."

"He probably doesn't talk much about it. There's a

chance that if I'd been more mature, we would have stayed together. To quote Mae again, 'Marriage is a great institution, but I'm not ready for an institution.'"

Odell laughed so hard that coffee sprayed out of his mouth. "I've gotta say, we've missed your humor. I really appreciate your coming on such short notice. Otis kept saying your name."

"I'm glad you called. Otis is a good man, and I would have been devastated if no one had let me know he's so sick. You and Otis ought to come up and see me some-time." Darlene fluttered her eyelashes and said the words just as they'd been uttered many years ago, and that's when I realized who Mae was. Darlene was talking about Mae West. I'd half-watched some old movies Daddy rented with Mae West and W.C. Fields. Darlene's ex-pression and intonation were exactly like Mae West's. She quoted the deceased actress a lot.

"I doubt you know what we're talking about," Odell said to me. "Darlene is a Mae West impressionist, but Mae West was way before your time."

"I've seen her on videos," I said.

Odell changed the subject and leaned toward Darlene, "You're welcome to stay with me or at Otis's place."

"No, I reserved a motel room right after you called."

Feeling they might want to reminisce, I finished my coffee and sandwich, stood, and said, "I'm heading home. Call me if there's any change, Odell, and it was nice to meet you, Darlene."

"Did you say Denise is forwarding calls from the mortuary to my cell phone?" Odell asked.

"No, to mine. They don't like you to use cell phones in the hospital. Don't worry. I'll come for you if we need you."

"Bye then," Odell said and went back to his second sandwich.

"Let me give you some advice," Darlene said. "More from Ms. West. She said, 'Love thy neighbor—and if he happens to be tall, debonair, and devastating, it will be that much better.'"

I didn't have the heart to tell her my nearest neighbor was my blind friend, who happened to be another female.

# Chapter Ten

Shouts blasted from Jane's side of the duplex when I opened my car door. No need to wonder who was making all the noise. A purple Ford 350 and Frank's old clunker were parked in Jane's driveway. I'd pulled in on my side. Big Boy was tied to the small oak tree in the yard. His howls mixed with the human yells. I unhooked the leash from the oak, bounded onto the porch, and opened the door into Jane's living room.

Thank heaven none of them were swinging fists. This was clearly a verbal argument that had full potential to turn physical, but hadn't yet reached that level. I didn't think either of my brothers would hit a woman, but they'd certainly fought each other in earlier years. I wouldn't put it past Jane and Molly to knock each other around if they got mad enough either. They all screamed at the same time. Big Boy lunged toward Molly, and Bill gripped the dog's collar, pulling him away as I tried to hold onto the leash.

"Get that dog out of here," Molly screeched. She added, "If it wasn't Jane's idea, why'd you even ask me?"

"They told me *you* wanted a double wedding!" Jane yelled.

"I'm all for it!" Frank shouted.

"Why not?" Bill demanded as he struggled with Big Boy.

He barked and howled alternately. I mean the dog barked and howled, not my brother. I picked his leash up from the floor and clipped it to his collar as Bill pushed the Great Dane onto the porch and slammed the door behind us.

When Big Boy finished squatting like he always does when he tinkles, I tried to take him for a walk. He pulled on the leash, jerking me toward the apartment door.

I tugged as hard as I could to urge him to the sidewalk, but he wanted no part of it. He pulled me up the steps to the porch. I opened the door just a few inches, stuck my head inside, and said something I never say. Something that would get a five-year-old three minutes in the time-out chair when I taught kindergarten.

"Shut up!" Several years of calling kids in from recess had boosted my vocal power even if I didn't use it much any more. Not that I'd ever told a child to "shut up." Buh-leeve me. I think *that* expression is totally and completely rude, but the four of them screaming at each other was just as bad and demanded an impolite response.

"Callie!" Jane exclaimed. "I'm so glad you're home. Send these people away, will ya?"

"One of them is your fiancé and the others will be your relatives after the weddings. What's going on?" It was all I could do to control Big Boy. He kept leaping toward Molly. *Could he remember her from living at her kennels when he was a puppy?*

Molly stepped away from the dog and shook her finger at me. "You told me to get the two couples together to discuss this double wedding business," she said. "Jane invited us over for supper, and it's just like you said, not Jane's idea to ruin my wedding. And unless the lipstick I found in Bill's truck belongs to you or Jane, there may not be a wedding for *us*."

"It's not mine," Jane said. "I haven't even seen Bill's

new truck." When I first met Jane, sight terms bothered me, but she uses them all the time. "See ya later" is her standard goodbye. When she said she hadn't "seen" the truck, she meant she'd neither been in it, touched it, nor had it described to her.

Molly held a Revlon tube of "Gypsy Rose" out to me. My hold on Big Boy barely relaxed for a second. He jerked away from my grasp and jumped toward Molly. I dang near died. My big old dog started humping Molly's leg like I don't know what. Bill grabbed the dog's collar, but Big Boy kept hunching. Panting and hunching. It took Frank and Bill both to get the dog away from Molly.

"I *told* you to tie that dog out front!" she roared.

"I don't ever tie him outside," I protested and tried to take Big Boy from Frank and Bill. The dog pounced toward Molly again. Bill grabbed the collar and forced the Great Dane back as his girlfriend jumped behind the couch.

"What's happening?" Jane usually keeps up very well, but there was no way she'd know exactly what my dog had been doing to Molly's leg.

"Put him in the bathroom," I ordered. "He's used to being shut in there."

Bill, Frank, and I shoved Big Boy in beside the tub. I didn't even take the tissue out like I usually did. This meant the dog would shred the roll into confetti. We just slammed the door tight and listened to Big Boy howl.

"I think I should leave now," Molly said, "but I need someone to give me a ride home. I'm sorry about dinner, Jane, but I'll talk to you later."

"You don't need a ride home. I brought you and I'll take you back." Bill said.

"Unless Callie tells me this is her lipstick, I don't want to set my foot or my behind in that purple truck *ever* again." Molly said.

Everyone turned to look at me. Even Jane faced me though she wasn't actually *looking* at me. *What should I do? It would smooth things over if I said it was my lipstick, but would I want anyone to lie to me about something like that?* Wordlessly, my brother Bill begged me with his eyes. He wanted me to cover for him.

I couldn't do it. I didn't say, "No, it's not mine," but I couldn't make myself claim the lipstick either. I remained silent.

"I guess that does it," Molly said. Tears streamed down her face. "Frank, will you take me home?"

"I really don't want to get into this," Frank mumbled.

I handed Molly my SpongeBob SquarePants key ring. "Take my car," I said. "I'll get someone to bring me to pick it up. Everyone needs to settle down and then talk this out calmly. No double wedding, but, Molly, that lipstick could have been left in the truck by a sales lady or by someone who took it for a test drive." Molly closed her hand over the keys and walked to the door. She looked back at me. "Thank you, Callie. Now let me tell you what to do. Be a responsible pet owner and get that dog *fixed!*" She paused. "And if I'd married your brother, I'd have needed to have him neutered, too."

Jane giggled. "I'd never marry anyone who'd been neutered. What would be the point?"

Frank's expression was unreadable. Surprise? Shock? Offense? I couldn't tell.

"What if you married someone and then he became . . ." Frank searched for the right word.

"Unable to perform his husbandly duties?" I offered.

"Duties?" Jane asked. "Duties? It's a privilege, not a duty."

"What about love?" Frank said. "Marriage is about more than privileges or duties. Wouldn't you still love me if I couldn't?" He looked directly at Jane, then added,

"Not that I'd ever have that problem."

I flopped down on the couch beside Jane. "What's wrong with my dog?" I asked, trying to change the subject. After all, I thought that particular conversation between Frank and Jane should be held in private. "He's never behaved like *that* before."

"What was he *doing*?" Jane asked.

I leaned over and whispered my answer in her ear.

Jane roared with laughter.

Frank said, "Well, it is Wednesday."

"What's that got to do with it?" I asked.

"Hump day," he said.

Jane chuckled but said, "You're *so* lame!"

"The truth is," Bill said, "that unless you plan to breed your dog, he does need to be neutered. He's so big and hard to handle. You'd have a real problem if that happened when you were walking him."

"Well, I've already spent a small fortune on him," I grumbled. "Besides buying his toys and special shampoo, I've had to pay to repair and replace a lot of stuff he chewed up when he was younger. He's had his ears cropped and all his shots and treatments, too. I'll call the vet and make an appointment or could I just get a farmer to do it like they do cows and hogs?"

"Just call the vet, would ya? Pa might own a farm, but none of us is gonna cut Big Boy's mountain oysters." Bill said, then turned the subject back to Molly. "What should I do now? Take her flowers?"

"You'd better have the florist deliver them in case she decides to take a whack at *fixing* you herself," Frank laughed.

"Whose tube of lipstick did she find in your truck?" Jane asked.

"I don't know," Bill said defiantly. "Like Callie said, it must have been left by someone who test-drove the truck before I bought it."

My brother was lying. I knew it, and from the expression on his face when he looked at me, he knew I knew. He had seen me at Taylor's Cemetery.

# Chapter Eleven

While Jane finished preparing Pimiento Chicken for dinner, Bill and I made our phone calls. Mine to Big Boy's vet to schedule an appointment for neutering. Bill's to St. Mary Florals to send Molly a bouquet of roses. Frank took the dog out of the bathroom and for a walk. Bill and I were sitting in the living room alone. It seemed a good time to ask THE questions.

"*Who* was that woman you were with over at Taylor's Cemetery today and *what* were you doing there?" I said.

"I thought that was you on the front row, but that wasn't a Middleton's tent."

"No, Odell's at the hospital with Otis. They subbed out setting up for the funeral to Clark's." Bill didn't comment. "What were you doing there and who was she?" I repeated.

"It was my friend Lucy, and we weren't *doing* anything. She'd heard I was getting married and just wanted to talk to me. Considering how jealous Molly is, I thought it would be best to go somewhere private."

"To a *cemetery?*"

"I know the place to park when you were in high school was the deserted Halsey farm, but when I was a teenager, the Halseys still lived there. The place to go was a cemetery. I chose Taylor's today because it's far enough from St. Mary that I figured no one who knew me would see us." He looked embarrassed. "How was I to know my own sister would catch me and then refuse to defend me."

"I'm not going to lie for you about something like that. If you still want to see other women, you don't need to be getting married."

"We were just talking, and I *do* love Molly and I *do* want to marry her."

"Sneaking off with other women isn't the way to show it. You're as big a hound dog as Big Boy."

"Oh, your dog's not that bad. Molly invited that behavior."

"What?"

"She told me on the way over here that she'd spent the morning breeding poodles. I doubt that she changed clothes before I picked her up. Your dog smelled the bitch on Molly. That's why he was so crazy."

"Then I can cancel the vet appointment?"

"No, unless you plan to breed him, you need to have him neutered. He'll be much easier to control."

"What are you going to do about Molly?"

"Once she gets the flowers, she'll listen when I tell her the woman who sold me the truck must have left that lipstick."

"You've gotta stop lying to her or break off the engagement." The minute I'd said it, I realized how ridiculous that sounded. He should stop lying to her whether they married or not.

Just as I began to expand on the subject, my cell phone rang. Caller ID showed the mortuary. Expecting a pickup call, I answered to hear Denise's frantic words, "Callie, the sheriff is here with the FBI. They want to see the body in the cooler. You know good and well that I'm not going in there to pull it out. I told you I'm not doing anything with dead bodies. You need to get over here now!"

"I'll be right there," I said and disconnected the phone before I remembered I'd lent my car to Molly. I turned to my brother. "Bill, I have to go the funeral home. Will you take me there or run me by Molly's to pick up my car?"

"Are you leaving?" Jane called from the kitchen as though she hadn't been listening to every word we'd said.

"Yes, I'll eat when I get back," I answered.

"Me too," Bill said as Frank came in with Big Boy.

"You too what?" Frank said.

"I'm taking Callie to pick up her car from Molly."

"Why now? Dinner smells almost done."

"It is, but Callie's got to go to the funeral home," Jane called from the kitchen.

"If you're in this conversation, come in here with us," Frank said.

"No, I can't," Jane replied in an irritated tone. "I have to stir right now. The sauce will lump if I come in there."

Bill and I didn't stay for the rest of this conversation. As he drove me to Molly's place, which was between the apartment and the mortuary, he attempted to justify sneaking off with another woman the month of his wedding. I tuned him out because none of it really mattered. If that meeting had been innocent, why was it so sneaky?

I went to Molly's door for my keys. She thanked me, looked over my shoulder, and beckoned Bill over. I drove away. Let them work out their own drama.

Sheriff Harmon knew me well enough to know I'd come in the back door. He and a well-dressed woman in a white silk blouse and a midnight blue skirt suit that probably cost more than my whole wardrobe waited for me in the rear of the mortuary. She had auburn hair pinned up in back and that natural look of women who know how to apply makeup that enhances their beauty without the cosmetics being noticeable. I tried for that look every time I cosmetized a female.

"Callie Parrish, this is Special Agent Georgette Randolph," Harmon introduced us. Her handshake was solid, but not finger-crushing.

"I appreciate," she began, "your coming in after your shift is over." I didn't bother to tell her that mortuary employees don't exactly work shifts. It's not like we're working on the other side of town at the underwear factory where a friend of mine says she "sews crotches" from three until eleven.

"What can I do for you?" I asked, already knowing from Denise's call that they wanted to see Mr. Joyner's body.

In a few minutes, we were in the cooler area, and I pulled out the tray with Mr. Joyner on it.

Agent Randolph opened the body bag and bent over, carefully examining the face. She pulled up the golf shirt and looked at the abdomen. There was a crescent-shaped blemish on the left side of his rib cage. "That's it," she said. "I want to make another set of prints, but with your prints and the birthmark, I feel confident this man is Johnny Johnson. When I first read the reports, I thought he would have had plastic surgery on his face and had that birthmark removed, but he didn't." She reached into her leather tote and pulled out another fingerprinting kit. At the rate we were going, we'd rub the prints off the body.

As she went through the printing routine, Agent Randolph said, "I'm going to authorize an autopsy, but he probably died of natural causes. According to our records, he'd be seventy-two years old now." When she completed the prints, she took a folder from her bag and showed the sheriff and me photographs of Johnny Johnson at the time he disappeared. Mr. Joyner had aged, but the features were still those of the robber.

"At this point," she continued, "we can close the case of locating Johnny Johnson, but we'll want to investigate whether or not any of the money is still around. Sheriff, didn't you say he has a wife?"

"Not legally," Harmon responded, "but he's been living with a woman who goes by the name 'Mrs. Joyner,' and she can't find his social security number or any formal identification."

I thought about it. "She did say that he paid cash for everything, but she didn't say if it's kept in a safe deposit box or hidden under their mattress."

"Well, if any of it's left, it belongs to the government, not to the widow." Agent Randolph assured us.

"Do you want me to contact Mrs. Joyner and have her come in to give permission for the autopsy?" I foolishly asked.

Agent Randolph looked at me like I'd fallen off a turnip truck. Sheriff Harmon's expression wasn't much better.

"When the FBI requests an autopsy," the sheriff said, "permission from the spouse isn't necessary."

# Chapter Twelve

Agent Randolph rode off with Sheriff Harmon, who had a big grin on his face. Right before they left, the FBI lady had supplied her own papers and signed them, authorizing an autopsy on behalf of the United States Government—ASAP. Wow! Who was *I* to argue with that?

"Do you want me to take Mr. Joyner to Charleston?" I asked Odell when he answered his cell phone.

"No, and I can't do it because I don't want to leave the hospital while Otis is in Intensive Care. Call Jake. If he's well, he can make the trip. He probably needs all the hours he can get this week anyway."

"Mr. Joyner's been here a few days and usually you send them out as soon as possible. He hasn't been embalmed. Is that a problem?"

"Callie, a body is never intentionally prepped before autopsy. It makes the medical examiners furious, so it only happens if the post mortem is ordered *after* a body has been embalmed. You've been around here long enough to know that."

"I guess so," I mumbled. "We don't have a refrigerated removal van or hearse, do we?"

Odell laughed. "No, we don't. Just tell Jake to turn the AC on high and hurry!" He was still guffawing when he ended the connection.

As usual, (well, as *sometimes* usual), I did as I was told.

Jake had barely headed out to Charleston when Sheriff Harmon came back. He still wore that big grin.

"What are you so happy about?" I asked as the notes of "The Old Rugged Cross" ended.

Ignoring my question, he asked, "Has anyone picked up the Jaguar John Doe from Charleston yet?"

"I doubt he's ready. We haven't received the results."

"Well, a copy of the report was just faxed to my office." The sheriff still had a grin. Now it was a silly one. He was antsy too, like he couldn't stand still."

"Did they identify him?" I asked.

"No. That's my job. Turns out not to be a heart attack though. It's homicide."

"Murder?" I sat down in an overstuffed burgundy velvet barrel back chair. Wayne remained standing.

"Yep, some kind of poison. Toxicology reports won't be in for awhile, but the preliminary reports are pretty solid. Poison is homicide or an accidental death, and I'm betting someone got rid of him intentionally."

"Are they sure it wasn't snake venom?"

"I don't think they're sure about anything except that he appears to have died from some kind of poison." Wayne looked antsier than ever, checking his watch every minute or so. "Anyway, have the John Doe's body brought back here. This is my case."

I looked up at him. "Why do you look so happy? You can't possibly be glad the man was killed." He grinned even bigger, and a thought crept into my mind. "Could your joy have anything to do with a pretty FBI agent?" I asked.

"Well, I *am* taking Georgette to dinner tonight." He looked at his watch again. "As a matter of fact, I need to get home in time to shower and change."

"Georgette? I thought she was Agent Randolph."

Sheriff Harmon chuckled. "She's fascinating whether

you think of her as Georgette or as Agent Randolph."

"Can she bake pies?" I teased.

"I don't know. I'll ask her at dinner."

The notes of "Jesus Loves Me" began as Sheriff Harmon opened the door. I followed after him and called, "I forgot to tell you. The John Doe's shirt matches the one Mrs. Joyner brought for her husband's burial."

The sheriff turned and looked at me. "A green golf club shirt?" he asked.

"Yep, exactly the same. That's coincidental, isn't it?"

"Callie, there are seldom any coincidences in crime, maybe in everyday life, but not in police work."

"I don't guess it's such a big deal anyway, especially considering they're both from Hilton Head, I guess it's not so far out."

"How do you know they're both from Hilton Head?"

I paused before answering. "I assumed so because John Doe was wearing that Hilton Head golf club shirt, and Mrs. Joyner said they live in Hilton Head." I thought for a moment. "I figured the man in the car was from Hilton Head before I even got close enough to see his shirt. A lot more Jags in Hilton Head than here in St. Mary."

"Thanks for telling me. It's a stretch, but they could have been friends. Mrs. Joyner might recognize our John Doe. I'll arrange to show her his picture." He glanced at his wrist. "I'll give that some thought. Gotta get to that shower now." He closed his car door, waved, and drove away.

I considered sitting down on one of the big white rocking chairs on the veranda to enjoy the weather. The day was a lot warmer than usual for October. I'd have to leave the door open to hear the phone though, and that's a big no-no at a funeral home. Doors and windows are *never* left unclosed. I decided to take the chance, but the minute I sat down, the landline rang. I pulled the door closed behind me and dashed to the office.

"Middleton's Mortuary. Callie Parrish speaking. How may I help you?"

"Yes, this is Liz Taylor." *Good grief! A prank phone call to a funeral home.*

"Yeah, and this is Angelina Jolie." I shot back.

"No, not the famous Liz Taylor. I used to be Liz Burns. You know, the Burns family that runs the St. Mary Vegetable Garden Spot, but I married Evan Taylor. He died and I need to talk to Otis or Odell.

I boast that I neither give nor take guilt trips, but I sure felt shame-faced about my rude response to a recent widow.

"Oh, I am *so* sorry, Mrs. Taylor. I really thought . . ."

"I *know* what you thought, if you thought at all, but you were wrong. Can I speak to one of the Middletons?"

"I'm sorry, Mrs. Taylor, but neither of them is here right now. I can have Mr. Taylor brought in and set an appointment for you to meet with one of the Middletons here to make arrangements."

"I guess that will be okay. Evan died at the Lazy Days Rest Home just awhile ago, and I really feel bad about that. I'd been taking care of him at home and it just got to be more than I could handle. I had him moved to Lazy Days just yesterday, and here he up and died today, but I want to bring him home."

"Now?" I asked.

"No, certainly not now! What do you think? Or do you ever think at all? I want him home after you fix him up, so our family and friends can come here for the wake."

Most folks have visitations at the church or mortuary these days, but here in the South, visitation or a wake is sometimes held in the decedent's home. I'd offended the woman again. This definitely wasn't a good day for me.

"I'm sorry. I just misunderstood." I tried to sound as contrite as possible.

"Is this Middleton's or an answering service? You don't seem to know much about the funeral business."

"I'm here at the mortuary. I apologize. I'm here to serve you. Middleton's will make every effort to help you through this difficult time." I was quoting Otis, and it certainly sounded better than when I spoke from my own mind.

"Okay." She sounded calmer. "Let's start over." She spoke very slowly and a little louder, the way I'd heard some people talk to Special Needs students when I taught. "My husband, Evan Taylor, has passed away," she continued. "He's at Lazy Days Rest Home, and I want Middleton's to handle everything. I want Middleton's to bring him home for visitation, then we'll have a service at the church the next day."

"Do you want him embalmed?" I asked. We always ask that question because prepping the body requires a signature. Besides, I guess I had Mr. Joyner on my mind.

"Of course I want him embalmed!" Mrs. Taylor said. "And I know from the last time that I have to sign to have it done. How late will you be open tonight?"

"We're open until eight o'clock, but I can certainly wait here for you if you want to come later."

"I'll try to be there before eight."

Now what? Usually pick-ups are made by Otis, Odell, or Jake. I've been on a few, but I rarely go by myself, and I really shouldn't leave before eight even though we didn't have anyone resting at the moment. That's not real Funeraleze. "Resting" is my own term for a body being on the premises—in the cooler, the prep room, or lying in a casket in one of the slumber rooms.

Odell was worried about Otis, and I'd already called

him several times. I made the decision for myself. I'd reached for the telephone to call Denise to come cover the phone while I picked up Mr. Taylor, when our other line rang.

I answered, "Middleton's Mortuary. Callie Parrish speaking. How may I help you?"

"This is Tessie over at Lazy Days Rest Home. I've called to report that Mr. Evan Taylor has passed away, and his wife specified that Middleton's is her funeral home of choice."

"Yes, she's already talked to me."

"Then will someone be here soon? I told her we'd call you, but Mrs. Taylor is the kind of woman who has to have her own way and insisted she'd call you herself."

She coughed softly. "Believe me, the poor man was only here one day and she drove us crazy with her instructions. More like demands that everything be done her way, even though we're professionals in caring for the ill and elderly."

I'd stopped listening when she said, "Believe me." It was the first time I'd heard an older woman use my favorite expression, even though she said it like, "b'lieve" and I say it, "buh-leeve." Of course, I had no way to know her age, but she sounded quite elderly. Like she ought to be a patient instead of an employee at Lazy Days Rest Home.

"Yes, ma'am," I said. "We'll be there soon."

"Bye," she said softly.

I called Denise and asked if she could come over and stay while I was out, explaining that I'd only be gone about an hour.

"Be there as soon as I get my dress on," she answered and for a moment, I wondered if I'd interrupted something before I realized she meant get out of jeans or whatever she was wearing and into her long-sleeved black dress.

The pick up went fine. An employee there helped me get Mr. Taylor into the body bag and on the gurney. I spread the cover over him before we moved to the hall. The sight of a body bag being wheeled out is disturbing to lots of people, especially the elderly and ill. I don't see where it matters a lot since they know what's under there, but rules are rules, and my bosses insist they be followed. All the patients' doors were closed as the employee and I wheeled Mr. Taylor to the service exit. As the orderly and I put Mr. Taylor into the funeral coach, a little lady who looked like the epitome of a true old fashioned southern lady came out to us.

"I'm Tessie," she said. "Are you the young lady I spoke with at the funeral home?"

"Yes, ma'am."

"I am *so* glad to get that man out of here. Not that I'm ever glad when a patient dies, mind you. I'm just glad that wife of his won't be back. She's tried to boss everybody here around since her husband came in. She was even telling employees who had nothing to do with her husband how to do their jobs. Thank you for taking him away."

She shook my hand and went back into the building.


Denise was sitting at my desk and shrieking when I walked into my office.

"What is going on around here?" she screamed.

"Nothing unusual that I know of," I answered and leaned across her to look in the message basket on my desk. "What's got you upset?"

"It's too noisy here. I'm not going to work this job after dark anymore."

"Been hearing the ghosties walking 'round?" I kidded,

and I didn't mean to. I promise I didn't mean to, but I raised my arms and moaned, "Whoooooo, whoooo!"

Denise put her head on the desk and sobbed.

"Come on," I tried to comfort. "This is an old house. If you've heard anything, it's the settling and normal sounds of the building. Besides, if there were such a thing as ghosts, I'd have seen one by now. I've been working here three years." Hoping that would pacify her, I changed the subject. "Have there been any calls?" There weren't any notes in the message basket, but if she'd been this upset, she may not have written anything up.

"Jake called. Told me he got a speeding ticket on the way to Charleston. No other calls, but a Mrs. Taylor came by. She said she needed to sign an embalming form and screamed at me until I found one in the bottom drawer of your desk. It's right here." Denise waved the paper in front of me. "There's a picture, too. She said she'll be here at ten in the morning for a planning session, and she wants to see Mr. Taylor then. She expects him home by tomorrow afternoon for the wake she's planning." Denise looked over her shoulder as though she'd heard something, but the room was silent to me. "Mr. Taylor's clothes are hanging in the entry. I didn't want to go into any of the rooms."

"That's fine." I said. Denise stood, picked up her purse, and briskly walked toward the door. "Wait up! You can't leave yet. I need you to help me," I called.

"I am *not* helping you unload that corpse," Denise said. "I told you and the Middletons when I came to work here that I'm not touching or working around anything dead."

"I know, Denise," I comforted. "All I want you to do is sit here and listen for the door or phone calls while I get Mr. Taylor into the building."

"How are you going to do that by yourself?"

"He's not very big, just a little old man. I can do it."
*Yeah, my mind told myself. You can slide him off the gurney onto the tray for the cooler, but you can't embalm him.*
*Better call Odell again.*

When Mr. Taylor was secured in the cooler and Denise on her way home, I called Odell and brought him up to date.

"I'll stay here until Jake gets the John Doe here," I said.

"No, Otis is doing better. I'll come in, prep the new gentleman, and wait for Jake. You can go home when I get there, but I'll need you in for cosmetizing in the morning."

"By the way, Jake got a speeding ticket."

"A speeding ticket! Why in tarnation would he go over the speed limit in the funeral coach?"

I tried to defend Jake. "Well, you did say to tell him to turn the air on high and hurry."

"I was teasing you," Odell growled. "I'll be there soon." As the call ended, I heard him mumbling, "Can't take a joke—can't even tell what's a joke and what's not."

# The Chapter Between Twelve and Fourteen

At last! For years I've avoided the number thirteen. I'm not really superstitious, but I don't push my luck. The only good thing about that number was some wonderful folks have been born on the thirteenth day of different months. Now—at last—a really good thirteen has entered my life.

After George Carter was dispatched (Isn't that a *sweet* synonym for "murdered"?) by Dennis Sharpe, who will probably spend the rest of his life in a mental institution, Phyllis Counts returned to South Carolina and won the Southern Belle Flour Baking Contest. She expanded her catering company from a home enterprise operating out of her kitchen and van by opening a retail outlet in Beaufort. The name of her shop is Baker's Dozen and she sells every kind of cookie I've ever heard of. If a customer names a cookie Mrs. Counts hasn't made, she'll research the recipe and bake samples.

What does that have to do with the number thirteen? A baker's dozen is thirteen, not twelve. I looked it up on the Internet. The original idea came from way back in the 1200s when bakers who short-changed their customers could receive severe punishments, like having a hand cut off. To be positive that no one was accidentally short-changed, the bakers gave thirteen for a dozen.

If someone orders a dozen of anything at Baker's Dozen in Beaufort, there are thirteen in the bag or box. Buh-leeve me. I've been seeing a lot of Mrs. Counts lately.

She says it's her way of showing appreciation to customers. I say the only thing better than twelve cookies is thirteen cookies, and the only thing better than thirteen cookies is thirteen Moon Pies.

Don't think this means that I've changed my mind about writing a chapter thirteen. I thought about it, but I'm going to limit my dealings with thirteen to making trips to Beaufort for snicker doodles. A Baker's Dozen— thirteen of them.

# Chapter Fourteen

*Dalmation!*

I'd rushed to get to work early and dress Mr. Taylor. As sometimes happens, the picture his wife left for me wasn't recent. The man looked about eighty, and the picture was of someone in his thirties. Mr. Taylor's hair, what there was of it, was snow white. The man in the picture had a head full of dark brown. Mr. Taylor had changed considerably, either from age or illness.

Denise hadn't said a thing about Mrs. Taylor wanting her husband's hair colored and I couldn't find a note about it. I called the widow.

"Good morning, Mrs. Taylor, this is Callie Parrish at Middleton's Mortuary," I began.

"How can you say 'good morning' to me the day after my husband died? Is this the same person I talked to yesterday?"

"Yes, ma'am, I did speak with you yesterday."

"That other girl, the one I gave the clothes to, is a lot nicer than you are. What do you want?" Before I could say a word, she rattled on, "You'd better not be calling to tell me I won't be able to see my Evan when I come in at ten. I've already invited everyone to the wake at my house tonight, and I want to be sure he looks right before you bring him out to the house."

"No, ma'am. Everything should be on schedule. In

the photo, Mr. Taylor's hair is darker. Do you want it tinted to match the picture?"

"Of course not! Just comb it the same way and use the makeup to make him look as much like the picture as possible. I've got to go now. I'll be in at ten o'clock, and I expect to talk to Mr. Middleton, not one of you girls!"

"Yes, ma'am." I disconnected the phone and got busy. By the time I'd finished the cosmetology part of my job, Odell was there and helped me dress Mr. Taylor. We couldn't casket him (Funeralese for positioning a body in the coffin) until Mrs. Taylor arrived and picked out the one she wanted.

My job includes handling obituaries, both e-mailing them to newspapers and posting them on our Internet announcements, but I couldn't do that either until plans were made. I pulled a new book from my desk—*Darkside of the Planet* by David Lee Jones. I knew David when I lived in Columbia before I moved back to St. Mary. Excited that his first book was published, I'd ordered it from Amazon.com and was eager to revisit my old friend through his writing. I settled in to read until Odell and Mrs. Taylor completed the plans.

When the phone rang, I answered like I always do: "Middleton's Mortuary, Callie Parrish speaking. How may I help you?"

"Look at the caller ID, Callie. It's me, Jane." I've told her hundreds of times that the proper pronoun is "I" as in "It is I," but Jane thinks "me" sounds better.

"Sorry about that. So you're up now?" I asked.

"Yes, I worked late last night. Roxanne was on the phone in my room when you came in. Did I keep you awake?"

"Not at all. You know that soft, whispery voice of Roxanne's doesn't come through the walls."

"Good. I told Frank that I'm going to do my job the

nights he's not here until we work things out. Do you think that's all right?"

"Jane, when have you ever needed my permission to do anything?"

"I'm just asking your opinion."

"It won't make any difference. You'll do whatever you want anyway. That's one of the things I like about you."

"Okay, I'm going to take that as a 'yes, it's okay' answer. Do you have to work all day?"

"Probably. Why?"

"I want to go shopping and buy something new to wear to that shower tomorrow."

"If I can get off work, I'll call you, but, Jane, you have lots of nice clothes."

"Yeah, I'll wear something I have if you can't get off early. I just want to look extra nice."

"Sure. I'll call and let you know. If we don't get to shop, I'll help you go through your closet tonight and pick out something smashing."

"Thanks." I heard her sniffle. Jane's not a person who cries easily, but by the time we'd disconnected, she was sobbing.

I was sitting at my desk reading David's book, when the door opened. Odell stood behind a scrawny, wrinkled lady with the brightest hair I'd ever seen. Obviously, this was not a Clairol or Redken dye job. None of the top brands make anything so brassy orange. She'd either colored it with Kool Aid or bought the dye from a dollar store. No, not a dollar store, a nickel or dime store.

"Well, would you look at that? Just what I would have expected. She's hiding and reading instead of doing her job." Her harsh tone matched her hair.

"Now, Mrs. Taylor, Callie works very hard here, and we're aware that she reads between chores." Odell.

"Well, I'd fire her!" Mrs. Taylor.

"Are you pleased with Mr. Taylor's appearance?" Me. Trying to be nice.

"He looks dead." Mrs. Taylor again.

"Here. These are the papers." Odell handed me the forms. "Let's get the obituary posted online and out to the newspapers. I've listed the ones Mrs. Taylor wants to receive notification." Odell. Nudging Mrs. Taylor back into the hall.

I put the book in a drawer and composed the obituary on the computer. I posted it online at the Middleton's website, then e-mailed it to the newspapers. I heard "Jesus Loves Me" on the sound system and assumed Mrs. Taylor had left, so I went to the entry to talk to Odell. Mrs. Taylor stood with him, and Mrs. Joyner had joined them.

"Hello, Mrs. Joyner," I said.

"So she does get off her behind sometimes," Mrs. Taylor sniped.

Mrs. Joyner gave Mrs. Taylor a surprised look. "I do hope it's all right with you. The sheriff called and wanted to drive to Hilton Head for me to look at some photographs. I told him I'd meet him here because I'd really like to see Harry again. I understand he's back from Charleston."

"Yes, ma'am," I said in the nicest, most courteous tone possible. "Would you like to see Mr. Joyner now?"

"Yes, before the sheriff arrives."

"Follow me," I said and led Mrs. Joyner down the hall.

"One o'clock," I heard Mrs. Taylor tell Odell. "One o'clock sharp!"

As Mrs. Joyner and I went to the cooler area, she asked, "Do you know what these photographs are about?"

I knew. What I didn't know was whether I was supposed to tell her. "I think," I said, "they're photographs of a man from Hilton Head. The sheriff wants to ask if you know this man or ever saw him with your husband."

"Why?"

"I'm not sure."

She didn't say anything else until I pulled Mr. Joyner from the refrigerated unit. His burial clothes had been removed and he was back in a body bag. I only opened the top so she could see his face.

Mrs. Joyner reached out and touched his cheek. "You know, I confess that when I first met Harry, I was very impressed with his money, but that changed. I learned to love him. He was a kind man." She stroked his face again. "Can you open the zipper all the way?" she asked.

"Not right now. Mr. Middleton has to dress him again."

"Oh, I understand."

I slid the drawer back into the cooler and Mrs. Joyner and I turned to leave the room.

"Mrs. Joyner?" the sheriff said as he met us in the hall. "I really appreciate your agreeing to this." He turned toward me. "Callie, may we use the front consulting room or is someone scheduled to be in there?"

"Help yourself. The room's available."

"May Callie come with us?" Mrs. Joyner asked.

"If that would make you more comfortable," Sheriff Harmon answered.

This was my first experience with a lineup, live or photo. I'd read about them in books, but I'd never been involved. When we were seated, the sheriff spread four prints on the table. I was surprised. Then I remembered this wasn't a lineup to choose one person from a group. The pictures were all the same person—the John Doe from the Jaguar. It was obvious that nothing had been done to take away the look of death. I don't know exactly how to say this, but he looked deader than he had in his car. I wished that I'd had the chance to cosmetize him before the pictures were made.

"Is he . . ." Mrs. Joyner began.

"Yes, he is," the sheriff said, "but we need to know if he's someone you and your husband associated with in Hilton Head. His name, if possible."

"I'm sorry, but I've never seen this gentleman before."

"Are you positive?"

"Absolutely, completely," Mrs. Joyner said, but her right eye twitched. I wondered if this could be a "tell" that she was lying like gamblers look for "tells" when someone is bluffing.

*No telling,* I thought when the sheriff and Mrs. Joyner left.

# Chapter Fifteen

"Ohhhhhhhhhh, I'm *so* glad you called me. I've been *so* hot thinking about you."

Big Boy jumped against me with his paws on my shoulders and licked my face the minute I stepped into the apartment. The words weren't coming from my dog. They were the breathy sweet purr of Jane's Roxanne voice. Jane had left her bedroom door open. As soon as she saw me, she walked over and closed it, still cooing into the telephone. Roxanne's 900 number is a separate line, but Jane seldom signs on to work so early in the evening. My guess was either she was running short of money or she was mad at Frankie. Probably both.

I pushed Big Boy down into a lying position and rubbed his belly with my toe. "Do you want me to cook?" I whispered when I opened her door slightly and peeked in. She batted her hand at me to go away.

After I changed from my black dress to jeans and a tee, I poked around in the cabinets to see what we had that might be simple and not require much effort or cooking skill. I was careful not to move anything. Jane's a good cook, but she depends on location for identification. That's why she always puts the groceries away. Her memory absolutely amazes me. I unload the bags and call out the name of each can or container as I hand it to her. She can put something in the cabinet and know what it is months later from remembering its position.

Jane could surely have created something fantastic out of a can or two, but I didn't see anything I wanted to try to prepare. I grabbed a Moon Pie and Diet Coke and sat down on the couch to watch television. Big Boy cuddled up beside me and I knew I should have made him move to the floor, but I appreciated his affection and fed him bites of my Moon Pie. There wasn't much on TV, and I wished I'd brought *Darkside of the Planet* home with me from work.

When the house phone rang, I answered, "Middleton's Mortuary, Callie Parrish speaking. How may I help you?" without thinking.

Odell laughed. "You may show up at work early tomorrow and handle things for me. Otis is doing better, but the doctors have scheduled a conference with me at one o'clock, which is the same time Mrs. Taylor wants Mr. Taylor carried to the house. She's having a home visitation tomorrow afternoon and a wake tomorrow night."

"Who's going to take him over there?" Usually, for a situation like this, Otis or Odell went with Jake or one of the other part-timers. When I came to work at Middletons, I thought several people would be needed to move a casketed body, but two men can do it. First, we have equipment that helps, and second, both Otis and Odell are very strong. I'm not going to say they've built muscles from handling bodies their entire lives, but that could be why.

"The only part-timer available is Jake, so he'll be going with you and staying throughout the night to represent Middleton's. I would have asked you to do that, but I know you've got that shower for your brother tomorrow and won't want to be up all the night before."

"I don't know if Jake and I can carry a casket into the house by ourselves. I'm not as strong as you or Otis."

"Of course not. I called your brother Frank and he's going to work part-time tomorrow to help you and Jake. Denise will be in at noon to take over the office."

"Did you tell Frankie to wear a suit?"

"I'd think Frank would know that, but, just to be sure, I told him. Keep track of his time and he'll be paid like any other part-timer. He says he'd like all the work he can get to help out with his wedding."

"You said Otis is better?"

"Yep, the doc tells me he can move out of ICU tomorrow if he continues to improve."

"I'm sure glad."

"Aren't we all?"

"Is Darlene still there?" I confess I'm nosey at times.

"She's here and says she's going to stay until Otis is well. Maybe even hang around and help out when he first goes home."

"Do you think they might get back together?" I found it hard to imagine Otis with a wife.

"No. I think Doofus has better sense than that. Darlene is a good woman, but she drove my brother crazy when they were married."

I didn't want to talk about that, so I said, "I'll be in at eight in the morning."

"Fine, and, Callie . . ."

"Yes."

"Try to get along with Mrs. Taylor. I know she seems difficult, but we must always remember that our services are for people at the worst times of their lives. I want your most professional appearance and courtesy."

"You'll have it. Will you call me after the conference with the doctors and let me know what they say?"

"You know I will."

"I'll take care of everything, Odell," I said and ended the call.

"What do you want to do for supper?" I asked Jane when she came out of her room.

"I can cook or we can go out. I wish the sub shop hadn't closed. I could really go for one of those meatball subs."

"There's nowhere in town to get that now. Do you want to ride to Beaufort?"

"No, let's just go to Rizzie's place."

Gastric Gullah isn't too far from our apartment and traditional food of the Low Country sounded good. With many apologies to Big Boy that he couldn't go, Jane and I hopped into the Mustang and headed for the best shrimp, oysters, and one-pot rice dishes in town.

Usually Rizzie greets me in the Gullah language. Growing up in the Low Country, I understand most of what she says. Tonight, she just called out, "Hey, I just made something brand new. It's got a lot of good food in it. Wanna try it?"

"Sure," I said. "Bring us two plates and one Diet Coke and one Dr Pepper."

"Gonna be bowls, not plates. It's got rice, but it's a little soupy."

"Fine. Just bring spoons," Jane said.

We'd hardly sat down when Jane whispered to me, "Can I talk about something private with you?"

"You know you can," I answered and looked up to see Rizzie standing by the table with two large bowls of a delicious smelling stew. Jane sensed her presence and stopped talking until Rizzie had gone back behind the counter.

"Wait just a second," I said. "She's headed back over with the drinks."

Rizzie set the glasses and a black cast iron skillet of cornbread on the table. We dug in, and Jane stopped talking. When we finished, I asked her, "What did you want to talk about?"

"Oh, nothing," she said in that way that means, "I've got a lot to say, but I've changed my mind about telling you what it is."

When we left, I drove around for a while, hoping Jane would open up about what was bothering her. She didn't say anything and went straight to her room when we got home. The slight sounds through the wall sounded like Jane might not have anything to say, but Roxanne talked all night.

# Chapter Sixteen

"Where were you and Jane last night?" Frankie demanded over "Blessed Assurance." He stood at the entrance to the mortuary wearing a black suit and looking too handsome to be my brother. I wondered if he'd bought the new clothes for his wedding. He had to rent a tux to usher for Bill and Molly, but Jane had already specified that, for her wedding, the men would wear dark suits they could wear again. As her only attendant, I was free to pick out my own dress. She didn't even care what color.

"What do you mean?" I asked and brushed a speck of lint off Frankie's shoulder.

"I mean I called Jane over and over, then went by the apartment and saw your car was gone. What were you two doing?"

"We were eating. Went over to Gastric Gullah. She'd fixed this stuff I've never eaten before, some kind of soupy shrimp and fish bog with okra and rice—scrumptious. You should try it if you're ever in there when she's made it."

"I don't think I need you to tell me what to eat at Rizzie's. Everything she cooks is fantastic. I *do* need you to tell me what my fiancée is doing. Callie, if she's sneaking around on me, I want to know. I think she's back working nights, too." He followed me to my office at the end of the hall. Denise sat my desk. I pulled open the side drawer and retrieved my purse. "I'll be back as soon as possible," I told Denise, then turned to Frankie as we left.

"Has she started acting Roxanne when you're at our place?" I asked. She'd never wanted me to listen in to her 900 calls.

"I'm not talking about when I'm there."

"Well, Jane's SSI isn't enough to support her. She needs to work somewhere, and that job pays well and doesn't require any transportation. The hours are flexible. It's got a lot of perks. Besides, she's already agreed to quit after you're married."

"I want her to stop *now!*"

"Frankie, that's between the two of you, but I can tell you this: Jane's not as happy as she was. She's moody and irritable most of the time. Is that coming from you or somewhere else?"

"I don't know. I love her, but I can't seem to make her happy."

"Do you mean . . ."

"No, I'm not talking about physical. She's seems withdrawn a lot."

"If I find out anything, I'll let you know. Right now, you can go to the loading dock and help Jake get Mr. Taylor into the hearse. I mean funeral coach. I have to load the van. Mrs. Taylor has requested that the most impressive floral arrangements be brought to the house. Then we'll deliver the remainder to the church tomorrow."

Odell had already given Jake directions, so we decided he and Frankie would lead and I'd follow in the van. When Jake turned through the gate to Magnolia Mobile Manor, I just about wet my panties. The Taylors lived in a trailer! Ex-scuuze me. Only rednecks call them trailers. The Taylor's lived in a mobile home. But trailer or mobile home, I didn't think we could get Mr. Taylor's casket through the door.

No need to worry about the number for the Taylors' address. The widow was standing on the stoop waving a dish cloth. Jake backed the funeral coach up to the front step as though fully confident the casket would fit through the door. I pulled the van in beside them.

"Bless your heart! You got here on time. When Mr. Middleton told me he wouldn't be able to come, I figured you'd screw it all up." She waved her hand toward the door. "Come on in and unload Evan. I want to be sure he still looks okay before any guests arrive."

"Pardon me, Mrs. Taylor," I said in my most professional funeral home voice. "We'll need to measure the door and be sure everything will fit before we remove Mr. Taylor from the hearse . . . I mean funeral coach."

"Do what you gotta do," Mrs. Taylor huffed, "but I assure you it will work." She sniffed. "I'll wait inside. Just let me know when you're ready. My friends took the couch out last night to make room for him." She slammed the door behind her.

Meanwhile, as they used to say in western movies, Jake whipped out two tape measures and handed one to Frankie. Jake climbed into the funeral coach and measured the dimensions of the casket while Frankie calculated the size of the front door.

If I were a gambler, I would've put money on the fact that Mrs. Taylor was ticked off. The look on her face, her tone, and her slamming the door—all indicated her mood. She was so sure that big casket could fit through the mobile home door. We run into that occasionally—people who think they know more about our business than we do.

Perhaps if she saw how beautiful some of the floral tributes were, she'd feel better. I opened the back of the van and pulled out a gorgeous wreath made of bronze fall flowers and yellow roses. I rang the doorbell, and she answered immediately.

"May I bring in some of the flowers?" I asked politely.

"Might as well. Those idiots will still be trying to figure out how to do this when my guests arrive. All they have to do is open the door as wide as it will go and tip the coffin just a little bit sideways."

I stepped into the mobile home. Mr. Taylor's spot was obviously against the picture window directly across from the entrance. I placed the wreath beside an end table. "Aren't those stunning?" I asked.

Mrs. Taylor ignored my question. "Can you please make them bring him on in?" she whined.

"There's some question about whether the door is wide enough." I answered. "We don't want to risk scratching the metal or damaging your door frame."

"Just hurry them up!" She nudged me toward the door. "Bring in the other flowers and we'll put them in the bedroom for now, then arrange 'em around Evan when those fools finally bring him in. This is ridiculous! Tell them I *know* it will fit. Just bring him in." She shut the door behind me.

Jake and Frankie approached me together. "We're not sure it will make it," Frankie said.

"We may have to take the door frame down," Jake added. "I'm worried about the body, too. Maybe if we take him out, then put him back in after we get the casket inside."

I grimaced. "And what are you going to do with him while you're trying to fit the empty casket through the door?"

Frankie grinned. "We could lay him out on that picnic table over there," he said and pointed across the yard.

If looks could kill, the ones Jake and I both cut Frankie would have made him need a casket himself.

"Mrs. Taylor insists that all you have to do is open the door completely and tip the casket a tiny bit," I said.

"And what makes you think she knows what she's talking about?" Jake demanded.

"I don't know, but maybe if we try it her way and it doesn't work, she won't be so angry about it," I answered.

Frankie couldn't resist getting in his two cents' worth. "And what if it tips too far, the lid opens, and the body falls out?" he asked.

"That won't happen," I said. "The lid is latched. Let's tell her we're ready to try her idea."

Mrs. Taylor beamed when we offered to attempt it her way before we began disassembling her door or removing the top of the casket. I'd hoped she would go into one of the bedrooms while Frankie and Jake worked, but she stood outside by the steps telling them what to do and able to see whatever fiasco happened.

I expected her to irritate the two men, and I didn't think a funeral floral piece would lift their moods at all.

"Now prop the door as wide as it will go," Mrs. Taylor instructed. Then, "You're going to have to tip it just slightly because the width is too big for the door, but if it's barely slanted, it will work."

I couldn't believe, I promise, I absolutely could *not* believe it worked. In hardly any time, the casket sat on its stand against the picture window across from the front door. When we opened the lid, Mr. Taylor looked exactly as he had when we left the funeral home. We brought in the flowers and arranged pot plants and baskets in front of the coffin with larger wreaths and sprays on each end.

When Frankie and I were finally free to leave, I told Mrs. Taylor, "Someone will be back in the morning with the funeral coach to pick up Mr. Taylor and Jake."

"Why is that young man staying? I don't need him for anything else."

"He can help out with whatever may be needed, or he'll just stay out of the way if you prefer."

"Why don't you take him with you?"

"State law requires that a representative of Middleton's remain with Mr. Taylor during visitations."

"But this is a wake."

"Same thing legally. Don't worry. He won't get in your way." I thought for a moment. "You know, Mrs. Taylor, that door does *not* look wide enough. How did you know exactly what to do?"

"I've lived in this trailer almost thirty years."

"I guess you've had a lot of furniture moved in and out in that long," I ventured.

"Sure have," she said, "but more important than that, Evan's death makes me a widow for the third time. I figured if Evan was the smallest of my three husbands, and the funeral people got the first two in here for wakes that way, it would work again."

Daddy says people need to learn to shut up and listen. Sometimes, life proves him right.

# Chapter Seventeen

*The night was clear and the moon was yellow,*
*And the leaves came tumbling down.*

But Stagger Lee was nowhere in sight.

That old song, one Daddy loved, echoed in my mind as I stepped out of my Mustang. The leaves were falling, but the night and moon parts didn't fit because it wasn't dark yet.

Molly's twin aunts lived on a working farm about thirty minutes from St. Mary. Having been very prosperous years ago, the family had built an impressive house on a hill top surrounded by pastures and fields. Not quite a plantation home, but close. The bridal shower was a cookout for couples. Molly's aunts had opened a drive-through in the fence around one of the pastures beside the long driveway from the road to the house. Signs directed guests to park inside the fence.

I'd heard the party would be pool-side behind the house. Even with the hot spell we'd been having, I doubted anyone would go swimming, but I felt over-dressed in my sundress and mid-heel, open-toed sandals. Most people wore shorts, and they kept looking at me. That could have been because my gift-wrapped present was so big that I could barely see around it.

Jane and I had planned to meet Frank and Bill at the

shower, but Jane was still mad at Frankie for questioning her when we got back from the Taylor home. At the last minute, she'd refused to go. Some folks might have thought that was jealousy on her part. After all, this was obviously a big deal for Molly and Bill. Jane's shower would be a simple affair for a few females, probably in our apartment since I'd be giving it. I knew better than to think Jane might be envious though. She was very secure in herself, and I'd never known her to be green-eyed toward anyone.

"Hi, Callie. Let me carry that for you." I peeked a-round the present and saw deep, molten eyes and crisp, dark hair. Even better was the big grin this hunk was wearing.

"Levi!" No need to fake enthusiasm. "I thought you moved away from St. Mary when the sub shop closed."

He lifted the package from my arms. "I did. What on earth did you buy? This thing weighs a ton."

"It's china. I told the sales clerk to finish out whatever they needed to complete four place settings. Buh-leeve me. It was every bit as expensive as it is heavy."

Levi nodded toward his chest. "My present's in my shirt pocket. I solved the problem with a gift certificate. Much easier to carry."

As we walked toward the two story, columned house with its neatly manicured grounds, I felt better than I had all day.

Levi and I had dated for a while when he lived in town and worked at a sub shop, but he moved back to Charleston, and gradually, the dates had grown farther and farther apart. I liked him. He was funny and charismatic— so charming that I wondered if he were a womanizer. I had a track record of being drawn to men who always said the right thing, men who were so captivating because they'd had lots and lots of practice.

None of that mattered right then. Levi and I were walking toward the house side-by-side, approaching the shower as though we were together. He even had on khaki slacks and a white open-collared shirt, which made my dress and heels suitable.

"What brings you back to St. Mary?" I asked.

"This party."

We'd reached the yard. More balloons and signs directed us to the back of the house.

Wow! Molly's aunts were trying to outdo the wedding reception. Humongous flower arrangements centered four long serving tables draped in white. Men in black pants, white shirts and dark rose cumberbunds circulated among the crowd with silver trays while others manned the grills. No hamburgers. No hot dogs. The succulent smells of steak and chicken. I glanced at the nearest serving table and saw steaks piled high on trays labeled in calligraphy— well done, medium, or rare. Barbecued chicken halves filled other trays. The female staff, dressed like the male servers, kept the tables full and neat.

My brother Frank called out, "Callie!" as he approached Levi and me. "Where's Jane?"

"She's not feeling well. You remember Levi, don't you?" I motioned toward him. "He was at my birthday party last summer."

"I remember. How you doing, Levi?"

"I'll be better when we find out where to put this box."

"There are tables over there," Frankie pointed out.

We maneuvered through the crowd toward a group of tables piled high with elaborately wrapped boxes and colorful gift bags overflowing with bright tissue. At least a hundred people milled around the pool and the food tables—balancing plates and picking at food and each other. No need to have worried about what I wore.

Clothing ranged from almost formal to bikinis.

"Can you believe bikinis in October?" I asked no one in particular.

"Can't beat a late hot spell on the South Carolina coast," Levi said and put the package on one of the tables. "I'll get us something to drink. What would you like?"

"White wine would be nice."

"Forget it," Frankie said. "They've got all this food— appetizers, trays of breads and meats, salad bar table, baked potato bar table, dessert bar table, but no bar. The only drinks available are lemonade and iced tea.

"I'll have unsweetened tea," I said.

"No, you won't. All the tea is sweet. Apparently that's how Molly's aunts like their tea."

I was glad he didn't add his personal opinion about this because just then Bill and two elderly ladies joined us. He wore gray dress slacks and a white shirt with a narrow gray stripe. The collar was open, and it struck a nice cross between dressy and casual.

The women were eighty years old if they were a day, but their eyes sparkled and each of them had a sprightly step. Like the guests in shorts and bikinis, the twins had dressed for the weather, not the calendar. They both wore flowered summer dresses, but thank heaven, they weren't dressed exactly alike. One wore shades of lavender; the other, shades of blue. My bosses, Otis and Odell, are identical twins, but Otis has hair implants and wears black suits while Odell shaves his head and only owns midnight blue suits. Molly's aunts had white hair, but their hair-dressers used different rinses. One was light blue while the other was pale lavender.

"Aunt Nina," Bill said and nodded toward Blue Lady. Then he gestured toward Lavender Lady. "Aunt Nila," Bill continued, "I want you to meet my sister Callie, her friend Levi, and my brother Frank."

The aunts smiled and offered handshakes to each of us. I immediately thought mnemonics—the way I'd learned students' names by creating associations when I was a teacher. Blue was Nina, both hair and dress. No connection there, but the "L" in Nila went with lavender.

Nina interrupted my thoughts in an exaggerated drawl, "Make y'allselves at home now and partake of all the food and drink. Molly is our only niece, and we want this to be a real party for her and Bill here." She motioned toward Bill. Like we didn't already know him!

Nila interrupted, "Ah just wanted this to be a touch of the Old South, a real southern gathering. We don't have many occasions to host social events any mo-ah. Ah tried to talk Nina into having a Mint Julep table, but she was afraid we might offend some of the Parrish family."

I dang near choked to keep from laughing. Alcohol in moderation does *not* insult anyone I know of in the Parrish family. Oh, Daddy doesn't believe I should drink because he treats me like I'm still a child, but the Parrish family members think a little alcohol, in moderation, livens up any gathering.

Bill moved on to introduce The Aunts to other guests. I call my five brothers The Boys, with capital T and B, because I don't think they'll ever grow up. I thought of Aunt Nina and Aunt Nila as The Aunts, with capital T and A, because they're unique. Good grief! Did I just relate Molly's aunts to T and A? I'm sure Daddy wouldn't think I knew what those initials stand for, but I did. The sisters weren't fat, but their soft pillow plumpness hid their figures. T and A weren't noticeable. They reminded me of one of the ladies in *Arsenic and Old Lace*.

"Come here, Calamine." No mistaking my father's voice. He sat at a little round table with two young people. He didn't look as much like a sixty-ish Larry the Cable Guy as he usually did. He was wearing khakis and an open neck light blue sports shirt. My brothers aren't always the brightest bulbs in the chandelier, but Frankie took advantage of our dad calling only me and turned the other way as I headed toward Daddy. Levi followed him.

"Megan! Johnny!" I shrieked when I recognized the kids. My niece and nephew from Atlanta! We hugged and I sat with them.

"Want me to get you some food?" Johnny asked in a voice that rose and fell with the tones I remembered from having listened to five brothers as their voices changed from child to man. Daddy and the kids had plates piled high.

"I'll go and be right back," I answered.

At the table, I lusted for potato salad and pasta salad, but I settled for tossed veggies and a small bowl of sliced fresh fruit. Of all the cheese and cracker selections, I chose brie and imported water crackers. No need to eat cheddar and Ritz. I keep that at home.

Back at the table, fifteen-year-old Megan said, "Aunt Callie, aren't you going to eat a steak?"

"I sure am. This is just for starters." I set the plate on the table. "Be right back. I need something to drink."

The tea and lemonade were being served from punch bowls. The line for tea was twice as long as the other, so I asked for lemonade.

A youngster about twelve years old had reached the front of the tea line. "Sorry," the server said, "Lemonade for you." She turned toward me. "Will you let her in front of you? We've been told not to serve tea to minors because of the caffeine."

I nodded, but the rationale seemed strange. It's not uncommon in the South to see toddlers drinking tea from baby bottles.

When I returned, John and his wife Miriam had joined Daddy and the kids. John was sitting in my chair, but he pulled one up for me. At first, I felt a little nervous around the couple. The last I'd heard, there were headed toward separation. Had they gotten back together or had they come as a family to tell the rest of us they were divorcing?

"Molly showed me the attendants' dresses earlier this afternoon," Miriam said to me. "That peach color will be so beautiful on you with your hair that shade of auburn, and I just *love* everything being in fall colors." *Peach?* I thought. *That dress is orange! I'm eating salad here because I don't want to look like a pumpkin!* I thought that but kept my mouth shut.

Daddy pulled a bandana from his pocket and swiped his brow with it. "If this heat wave doesn't let up, they need to change the colors to red, white and blue because it feels like the Fourth of July."

"Surely the heat wave will end before the wedding. It's the end of the month, isn't it?" John asked.

"October thirtieth," I agreed, thinking, *those pumpkin-colored dresses would have been perfect for a Halloween wedding.*

"Where *is* Molly?" Daddy asked.

"I saw Bill, but not Molly." Me.

"She told me she'd be a little late." Miriam. "She wanted Bill to wait and come with her, but he insisted on being on time because most of his friends wouldn't know Molly's aunts." She looked at my plate. "I'm going to get some salad," she said and turned toward Bill. "Do you want to come with me?"

"Sure," he said, "but I think I'm going to skip the vegetables and go for steak and potato. Want me to bring you back a piece of chicken, Callie?"

"No, I'm not that food-conscious today. Bring me a steak—medium."

We chatted as we ate. Megan and Johnny told Daddy and me about their schools this year. Megan was excited that she'd soon be old enough for her driver's permit.

*Ker-splash!* I assumed one of the guests in bathing suits had braved the pool, but

Johnny broke into loud guffaws and pointed over my shoulder toward the sound. I turned to look. Some of the guests had ganged up and thrown Bill in—fully clothed. He spluttered and came up laughing. Just then, Molly made her entrance down the back steps of the house. She held two poodles, one in each arm. Either poodles come in orangey peach or she'd had them dyed to match the attendants' dresses for the wedding.

"Bill!" she screamed. "What are you doing?"

"Just a little horseplay going on," Bill said with a grin on his face as he climbed from the pool.

Molly began a tirade, but she stopped midstream when a uniformed sheriff's deputy stepped up behind Bill's two friends who'd thrown him in the pool and began snapping handcuffs on them.

"What do you think you're doing?" one of the men asked.

"Arresting you for creating a disturbance and probably for public drunkenness," the deputy said, and I recognized the voice. Fast Eddie Blake had struck again.

"How about I take you in for public stupidity?" Sheriff Harmon said to his deputy as he popped up beside him. "This is a party on private property, and this is none of your business," he added.

"But Sheriff," Blake spluttered.

"Get the cuffs off and get out of here," Harmon barked. "I should never have let you stop by with me, whether we were going up to my fishing cabin or not."

One of the servers handed Bill a large, fluffy towel. "It's okay," Bill laughed. "I think I did something worse at my friend Bo's wedding. Let's call it even."

"Sorry," Harmon said and left with his new deputy by

his side, jabbering all the way.

As they passed me, Harmon leaned over and said, "I think we have an ID on Snake Man in the Jag. Call me when you leave here." I stood to follow him, but he waved me back to my seat.

Molly hurried Bill into her aunts' house, and soon they returned with Bill wearing khakis and a brown and white polo shirt. I wondered if Molly carried around an extra set of clothes for Bill like new moms do for their babies. Together, they circulated around the yard, speaking and laughing with their guests. I really wanted to see the gifts, but apparently, at high falutin' showers like this, the presents aren't opened until the end. Maybe even after the event is over.

I noticed that the guests seemed to be getting happier and happier. The crowd was full of tomfoolery and laughter. When Bill and Molly reached our table, Molly was most gracious to everyone. She and Miriam seemed to have bonded because they were discussing wedding plans as though Miriam had helped Molly with them from the beginning. So far as I knew, today was the first time they'd met. Some women go ga-ga over weddings and babies. I'm not a whole lot into either.

While we sat there, Molly picked up Bill's glass and took a sip.

She quickly turned away and spewed tea all over.

"What *is* this?" she squealed."

"Tea," said Bill.

John took a sip. "Long Island Iced Tea?" he questioned.

Daddy took a sip. "Nope," he laughed. "It's St. Mary Iced Tea—good old southern sweet tea with a healthy splash of grain alcohol."

"*What*? Did you add something to your drink?" Molly.

"Nope, it's right out of the punch bowl." Bill.

"No wonder Aunt Nila didn't make any sense when we talked to her." Molly in a panic. "She's drinking spiked tea and she's an alcoholic." Molly jumped up and looked around. She headed toward the plump little lady in the lavender floral dress. Bill followed her. They had almost reached Aunt Nila when she looked at them. Her eyes bugged as she saw them head straight for her. She turned and tried to go around the pool to the house, but the deck was too crowded with people, and the elderly lady wasn't steady on her feet.

When his friends threw Bill into the pool, he'd made a loud *ker-splash*. When Aunt Nila fell, there was no big noise. She just slid into the water. Automatically, I jumped up, but Bill had seen her and dived in beside her. He was lifting her out before I could even get around the table. He stretched her out and looked like he was going to do CPR, but she coughed and sat up. Molly was raising Cain. I couldn't tell what she was saying, but I could see that she was having one of her temper tantrums. I'd seen her do that before.

Aunt Nina pushed through the crowd around them and bent over her sister. Now she appeared to be fussing, too. I thought they should be more sympathetic. Aunt Nila lived in a house with a pool, but that didn't mean that, at her age, falling in was reason to scold her instead of offering sympathy and comfort. Once again, a server appeared with a big white towel, which Bill used to wrap around his future aunt while they helped her to the house.

I spotted Levi in the crowd standing around the pool. He was beside Loose Lucy, my brother Bill's friend who had been hiding out with him at the cemetery. Lucy's arm slinked around Levi, and I wondered if the reason he'd come to the party was to be Lucy's escort. Maybe Lucy felt she needed a man by her side at a wedding shower for a man she'd cheated with. Levi certainly hadn't made any effort to rejoin me since I came over to Daddy's table.

"Looks like Bill is marrying into an interesting family," John commented.

"Molly's marrying into one, too," Miriam said. "I can vouch for that."

"Now, Miriam," Daddy interrupted, "you're not saying that the Parrish family is anything less than perfectly normal, are you?"

Miriam smiled at him. "I'm not saying that because I've been in this family for years, and I hope to stay a Parrish 'til I die." Well, I hoped John had worked out his feelings of being ignored at home, because Miriam wasn't hesitant to reach up and kiss him when she finished talking. He grinned.

"Pa, would you care for some of that iced tea?" John asked Daddy.

"Don't think so, but let me tell you a secret." John leaned his ear toward Daddy, and the rest of us didn't hear what was said. I watched John when he stopped by the drink table and got two empty cups. He headed toward the edge of the yard, and I lost him in the crowd. A little while later, he returned and gave Daddy one of the cups while he sipped from the other. I wondered if there were another drink table somewhere else in the yard.

Johnny complained that John didn't let him and his sister bring their swim suits. "I'm bored," he said in that squeaky adolescent voice.

"Get something to eat," Miriam suggested.

"I'm already full," he complained.

"I've had about all of this wedding shower I can stand," Daddy said. "The kids can ride to the house with me. Pick them up when you leave." Johnny and Megan beamed. They didn't get to see their Grandpa much, but grumpy though he was with everyone else at times, he'd always been a doting grandparent to his only two grandchildren.

"I'll walk out with you," I said. "I worked until an hour or so ago, and I'm tired." I air-kissed Miriam and John on their cheeks.

As we walked through the crowd, we passed my brother Mike. Daddy asked him if he was drinking tea.

"No, not me," Mike said. "I've had a headache all day. Afraid that tea wouldn't mix too well with my migraine medicine."

"Why don't you go home with us?" Daddy asked.

"I've got to help Bill with some things, but I won't be late," Mike answered.

Daddy and I walked the kids around to the front of the house and up the drive to the entrance to the parking lot pasture.

"Are you spending the night?" I asked Megan.

"No, but we're coming back for the wedding."

The heeled sandals had gotten to me. I slipped them off and walked bare-footed with my purse in one hand and shoes in the other.

I knew what it was when I felt it. Growing up on a farm, I'd felt that sickening squish between my toes before. I stopped and held my foot up.

"Oh . . ." I almost slipped away from kindergarten cussing and said the "s" word.

"That's what it is, all right," Daddy said. Megan looked sympathetic. Johnny laughed, danced around, and made disgusting sounds.

I tried cleaning my foot off with some tissues from the car, but the smell was still there on the way home. I even forgot to call Sheriff Harmon.

If I ever have children, I want girls, not boys, and I don't want a pasture for the parking lot at my baby shower.

# Chapter Eighteen

7:16 flashed in red on my digital clock when I opened my eyes Sunday morning. The jarring ring of the telephone ended my hope to sleep late. It also brought an abrupt closure to whatever I was dreaming because the details fled when I awoke. With The Boys for brothers, it's a wonder I hadn't received a call like that long ago.

"Hello," I managed while Big Boy stretched his legs out and rolled around on the bed, flopping a paw in my face.

A recorded female voice responded, "You have a collect call from . . ."

"Mike Parrish." My brother's voice spoke his name.

". . . at Jade County Detention Center," the recording continued. "Do you accept the charges?"

"I do." Oops! Those are two words I'm not sure I'll ever want to say again. "I—I will. That's what I m-m-mean," I stuttered. Big Boy bounded off the bed and headed out of the bedroom.

"Callie? Callie? Are you there?"

"Yes, Mike, I'm here. Are you at the jail? Who's been arrested? Is it Daddy? Or Bill? Or Frank?"

"No, it's me. Now don't start fussing. Just listen. There's a long line of dudes behind me waiting for this phone, and I don't wanna make 'em mad. I need you to get some cash money. I don't know how much, probably several hundred dollars. Bring it to the county jail and be here by nine o'clock for my bail hearing."

"I don't *have* several hundred. I've got about twenty in cash, and I can go to the ATM, but I probably don't have even a hundred dollars in my account."

"Get it from Pa. Just don't tell him what you want it for."

"Yeah, you want me to call Daddy and ask him for a few hundred dollars, but I can't tell him why I need it?" Big Boy returned, carrying his leash in his mouth. I patted him on the head and whispered, "We'll go out in just a minute," before turning my attention back to Mike.

"Why were you arrested?" I asked my brother.

I could hear male voices complaining in the background.

"Hurry up!"

"You've had long enough."

"We need to use the phone."

"I gotta go," Mike said. "Get the money and be here by nine." He paused, then added, "*Please!*"

I dropped my sleep shirt on the floor and slipped on underwear, jeans, T-shirt, socks, and Nikes. Big Boy dragged me to the door when I clipped his leash to his collar. His business didn't take long, and I didn't bother taking him for his walk.

Back in the apartment, I knocked on Jane's door and called, "I'm going out. Be back as soon as possible."

Jane either didn't answer me or mumbled so softly that I couldn't hear her. I grabbed my cell phone and hit automatic dial for Daddy's number while I fired up the Mustang.

"Hey, Callie," Frank answered. I was surprised he was at the home place. It seemed that recently he was in the apartment with Jane whenever I woke.

"I need to talk to Daddy," I said.

"Well, good morning to *you* too," Frank snapped.

I heard the phone drop onto a table or some other hard surface as Frank yelled, "Pa, it's Callie. She's gotta talk to you!"

"Calamine?" Daddy's voice growled, making him sound like Odell.

"Daddy, I've got a problem, and I need you to help me without asking questions."

"What is it? Is your car broke down?"

"No, I need some money, a couple hundred dollars. Can I pick you up and take you to the ATM? I promise you'll get it back, but I don't want to tell you why I need it."

"Are you in trouble, girl?"

I didn't know how to answer. Finally, I said, "Kinda, but the money will get me out of trouble."

"Come on by the house. I've got about four hundred stashed in the back of my gun safe. You can take that, but I want it clear that it's a loan, not a gift."

"Yes, sir."

I turned on the radio and sang along with Carrie Underwood and Rascal Flatts as I drove to Daddy's house. As always, the long driveway was picture postcard beautiful. Old live oaks lined both sides. Their branches, loaded with lacy Spanish moss, dipped over the road. Abruptly the drive ended at the ugly farmhouse where I'd spent my childhood. When Daddy had grown tired of having to paint the outside every few years, he'd installed vinyl siding. The supply store had a really depressing dark gray on sale. Our house was gray with black trim and a black roof. Not dove gray. Angry thunderstorm sky gray.

I didn't have time to get out of the car before Daddy came out on the front porch.

He had one fist balled up, and I wondered if someone had made him mad. He hugged me, then opened the fist over my hand. Greenbacks fell from his palm to mine.

"That's three hundred, eighty-five dollars there. I hope it's enough for your problem." He looked down at the ground and blushed. "This isn't anything female, is it?"

"Oh, no, Daddy, I'm not in that kind of trouble."

"Okay, because times have changed, and you'd be welcome to move back in with me with a grandbaby. John's younguns are too far away for me to be a real grandpa to them. Besides, those kids are about grown. Did you see how big they are yesterday?"

Now it was my turn to laugh. Buh-leeve me. If that had been my problem, it would have been an immaculate conception. My love life had been nonexistent for months and months. At least Daddy didn't seem to know that. He'd probably be glad if he did. After all, I was over thirty and divorced, but he still thought I was too young to drink a beer. Sometimes I wondered if he thought I was a virgin, too.

I shoved the money into my jeans pocket, kissed Daddy on the cheek, and headed toward the Jade County Detention Center.

My experience with jails and prisons had been limited to television shows. I knew the directions to the new building, but I'd never been there. A sign on the dirt road pointed me to turn left. A parking lot at the end of the drive faced a large brick building surrounded by a chain link fence topped with rolls of razor wire. The enclosure wrapped up to the door on each side of the entry sidewalk so that it wasn't necessary to get into the fenced area to go into the building.

The first room I entered was a small lobby. About fifteen plastic chairs bolted to the tiled floor were crowded with men, women, and children. Some of them held magazines, but most of them just sat there, looking tired and bored. A baby cried, and the mother was busy un-buttoning her shirt, preparing to nurse him.

A young woman sat behind a desk in the corner and looked at me expectantly. "May I help you?" she asked.

"Yes, ma'am. I hope so," I said. "My brother called and asked me to come bail him out."

"What's his name?"

"Michael Earl Parrish."

"What's the offense?"

"I don't know."

"Well, they'll tell you around at the hearing." She motioned toward a door to the right of her desk. "Go through there," she said. "Follow the signs. You'll see a wall of lockers. When you get to them, put your purse and anything else you're carrying into a locker. The key will have a clip on it for you to attach it to your shirt, then go through the check point. The attendant will give you an ID to wear while you're in the back. Pin that beside the key."

"Will that be where I pay his bail?" I asked.

"No, you'll be going to the hearing where the judge will either set bail or deny it. If he sets it, someone will direct you to the cashier."

I followed directions. On the other side of the door, before I reached the lockers, I passed rows of people sitting in little cubicles.

After securing my purse and car keys in a locker, I walked through another doorway, picked up an identi-fication tag and followed the hall to an open area filled with people. An older, uniformed man holding a clipboard stood in front of a double door. "May I help you?" he asked.

"My brother asked me to be here at nine."

"What's his name?"

Once again, I identified Mike by his full legal name.

The guard looked at the paper on the clipboard. "Yes, we have him on the docket for this morning. Have a seat over there. When we call his name, you go into the courtroom and stand by his side. Do not touch him. Do not speak to him."

"What about the bail money?" I asked.

"Take it one step at a time, little lady," he said and pointed toward an empty seat on a bench by the wall.

When I sat down, the young woman sitting beside me said, "Hi, honey. They gotcha husband?" At first, she sounded like some kind of severe southern accent. Then I realized what it really was—she whined.

"No, it's my brother."

"I told my old man not to go out last night, but nothing would do but he had to go get some more beer. Sure enough, he's got *another* DUI. Driving Under the Influence will take your license, give you a big fine, and make you have to get expensive insurance in this state. Since it's not my old man's first offense, he may wind up in jail this time. Is that what they got your brother for—DUI?"

"I don't know, but I saw him last night, and he wasn't drinking. He'd had a bad headache yesterday and was drinking lemonade."

"You'll find out when you go in. They call out the charges," the lady said.

"What's the routine here? I've never done this before," I said.

"I been down here so many times I could do it in my sleep," she answered. "You'll go in there and stand by him. That's supposed to show the judge that he's got family. The judge will say what the fine or bail is unless they're going to keep him. If they don't jail him, they'll process him and call you to the cashier. You'll pay whatever it is or sometimes they let you set it up in payments. Then you take him home until his trial comes up."

"This isn't the trial?"

"No, unless they got him for something that's just a fine, he'll have a trial later."

The guard called a name and Whiney jumped up and ran to the double doors. They must have decided to keep her husband or set his bail really high because about ten minutes later, she came out crying and walked away without speaking to me again.

I sat on that bench for almost two hours before the guard called, "Michael Earl Parrish."

First sight of Mike standing there in an orange jumpsuit made the whole thing real. My brother had been arrested. He looked miserable. The guard led me to Mike's side in front of the judge's bench. The person I assumed was the bailiff said, "Michael Earl Parrish. Charged with driving with an open container of alcohol and failure to secure seat belt."

"Mr. Parrish," the judge said, "I see that you aren't charged with a DUI because the breathalyzer test indicated that you hadn't been drinking. Is that correct?"

"Yes, sir."

"Please explain the circumstances."

"My brother Bill's getting married. Last night, we went to a cook-out shower for the couple. Another of my brothers had hidden a keg of beer in the woods behind where Bill's fiancée's aunts had the party. When I loaded the keg into the back of my truck to take it home, it bounced around because the dirt roads were bumpy. I stopped and put the keg inside the truck on the passenger's seat. The seat belt lock is broken on the passenger side. I locked the passenger seat belt around the keg and fastened it in my lock. That's why I couldn't wear my own seatbelt."

I tried not to smile at the picture that surfaced in my

mind, but several others in the room grinned.

"Did the deputy tell you why he pulled you?"

"No, he just said that the keg was an open container since I hadn't removed the faucet from it."

"Okay, Mr. Parrish. I'm prepared to fine you one hundred dollars or I'll release you on personal recognizance and you're entitled to a trial on these charges."

"Your Honor, I appreciate the PR, and I'd like to request a trial by jury."

"That's your prerogative, but the time to do that is when your trial comes up. You'll be notified." The judge turned toward the bailiff. "Return Mr. Parrish to holding until processing is ready for him." He smiled at me and said, "You may go back to the front lobby. Your husband will join you there after he's been processed."

"Brother," I said.

"Pardon?"

"He's my brother, not my husband."

"Oh, well. Just go back and wait for him." He turned to the bailiff and said, "Next," as a deputy led Mike away.

# Chapter Nineteen

Three hours in a plastic chair in the county detention center lobby both bored and educated me. My brothers always considered school boring. I, on the other hand, enjoy learning about lots of things, just not about the Jade County jail.

I'd always assumed that visiting loved ones in prison might be almost as bad as seeing them in the hospital or even at my place of business. Not so. Sunday must be the most popular day for visitation. Families came in with everyone dressed up in their church best.

The waiting area was the same small lobby I'd been in before. I could see cubicles with stools facing television screens. The desk attendant spent her time registering visitors and calling names of who was next to talk by telephone with a prisoner on one of the video screens. There were obviously cameras on both ends because parents kept holding up kids in front of the screens. I was sad to watch men holding little ones up in front of the cameras for female prisoners to see their offspring. Seems to me that if a woman has a young child, she oughta be able to stay out of jail and raise her kid, but who am I to talk about that? I've got no experience with jail or kids.

The busy clerk had no time for my questions about when Mike would be processed, why was it taking so long, and was she sure I was waiting in the right place.

When Mike finally came around the corner, I jumped up and walked beside him through the door, down the walk, away from the razor wire and to my car in the parking lot. Mike must have taken that "You have the right to remain silent" seriously. He didn't say a word.

As we drove away, I asked, "You feeling okay?"

"Headache's better, but I've spent the night in jail with a bunch of drunks, gang members, and thieves. How do you think I feel?"

"Well, it's over now. How about lunch? Want to go somewhere?"

"Sure. I didn't drink my mud coffee nor eat my jail-house grits for breakfast. Let's go to your friend Rizzie's place, but first I need to stop for a whiz. I wasn't about to use the toilets in that place."

We stopped at a gas station and went to the side-by-side restrooms. I was about wash my hands when I heard Mike's voice.

"Callie? Callie? Can you hear me?"

"Yes, where are you?"

"In the men's room next door. I can *see* you!"

My jeans were pulled up and zipped, but I grabbed them anyway.

"How?" I asked.

"I'm poking my ballpoint pen through the hole. Look for it."

Sure enough, I saw the end of a pen sticking through a picture of a boat hanging on the wall. I grabbed it and wiggled it.

"That's it," Mike said. "Put your eye up to the hole." He pulled the pen out and I peered through the opening directly into one of his blue eyes. "Meet me outside," he said.

We came face to face by the water cooler between the two restroom doors.

"Should we tell the cashier?" I asked.

"No, he may be who made that hole."

"What should we do?"

"Let's go on to lunch. We can call Sheriff Harmon and tell him about it."

Barely a mile from the filling station, I saw a Jade County Sheriff's Department car parked on the shoulder of the road. I pulled over and was ready to get out, but the deputy was faster. He was leaning into my window before I got my door open, and he wasn't anyone I wanted to see. It was Fast Eddie Blake.

"License and registration," he said.

"I just wanted to report that back at the station, there's a hole in the wall between the men's and women's restrooms. You can see from one to the other. That's gotta be illegal, isn't it?"

He tapped his ticket pad with a pen, and repeated, "License and registration, please."

I handed him both and continued, "Don't you want to know which station it is?"

"Young lady, you were speeding. You can't distract me by trying to tell me some cock and bull story about some guy watching you in the truck stop restroom." He was steadily writing.

"There's no truck stop around here, and it wasn't 'some guy.' It was my brother!"

"That's perverted," he said as he handed me the ticket. I wanted to tell him off or slap him. Instead, I signed the ticket and hoped the judge would be someone I knew, maybe even someone whose beloved relative I'd cosmetized. From the few times I'd seen Blake, I knew arguing with him would be a waste of time.

I waited until Blake had pulled away in the patrol car, then edged back onto the road.

"Do you know him?" Mike asked.

"He's a new deputy named Eddie Blake. He came to the bookstore when I found that dead man, and Harmon sent him over to the funeral home when the FBI agent was there."

"That's the deputy who arrested me. I'm going to get a lawyer and burn him. I wasn't speeding or swerving or anything. That idiot pulled me for no reason. Furthermore, he impounded the truck as well as that keg and spigot. I'll have to pay a tow charge and storage for the truck. He'll probably hold the keg as evidence and I'll have to pay for it and the tap as well as losing my deposit."

"Daddy lent me the money to bail you out," I said, "but you'll have to repay me because you know he's not going to forget it. You'd better think about that before you go hiring a lawyer."

The seriousness of the situation seemed to settle over both of us, and we rode silently until we arrived at Rizzie's Gastric Gullah. Seems like I eat there more than at home.

An SUV with a trailer was parked directly in front of the building. The car on the trailer behind it caught my eye just as Mike let out a long, low whistle. "What year is it?" I asked.

"A '76, and she's a beaut," Mike said as I parked the Mustang. I'm a little vain about my car because my ex-husband Donnie won a few trophies with it in classic car shows before he did what he did that made me divorce him. The judge kindly let me take the car. My Mustang could have been a beat-up bicycle compared to the pristine Corvette with its paint sparkling in the sun.

Corvettes were out of my family's league and even my ex-husband's wallet. This one was white—a sleek, smooth machine with a custom paint job of an American flag blowing in the wind. The car itself, motionless on the trailer, looked like it was flying.

I think Mike could have stood there staring all day,

but I needed coffee and food. I grabbed his hand and tugged him toward the door.

"Fine um whar you will," Rizzie greeted us when we went in. Both Mike and I knew that meant to seat ourselves—find a table wherever we liked. Rizzie was to women what that Corvette was to cars. She was sleek and superior. Tall with dark skin, shiny black hair clipped close, beautiful midnight eyes with long lashes, voluptuous legs and bosom. All of that topped off with a generous smile that showed perfect teeth.

"I've got fresh oyster pie today," she dropped the Gullah language.

"Two of those and two coffees," Mike said, then asked, "Did you see the car out front?"

"No," Rizzie peeked out the front window. "Mmmm! I'd marry a fellow who drove a car like that."

A man sitting at the counter spun around on his stool and faced us. He grinned a big, beautiful smile and said, "I ain't lookin' for forever, but if you're interested in dinner and some dancing after you get off, I'm right here."

Rizzie blushed. I promise, as dark as her skin is, the redness shone bright. "Sorry, mister, I don't get off. I own this place so when I close, I have to clean up and shut it down."

"You've got a juke box. Mighty fine one from what I've seen. We could just have us a dance right here. Push the chairs and tables back and make us a little dance floor."

Mike and I sat down at a booth. I took a closer look at the man sitting at the counter. He was tall, well-built and had sandy brown hair. Nice features and an aquiline nose with blue eyes. For a moment, I wished Mike weren't with me. Didn't want him back at the jail, just not with me. Would the stranger have flirted with me if I'd been alone? He had no way to know that Mike was my brother.

Probably figured we were in a relationship instead of just related.

Shyness not being one of my main virtues, I looked directly at the stranger and asked, "Is that gorgeous 'Vette out there yours?"

"Sure is." He took a sip from the glass beside his bowl of shrimp and grits. "I'm on my way from Florida up to a car show in Charleston and decided to detour off 95 and swing through St. Mary. I haven't been here in years."

He was one gorgeous hunk of man, but something nagged at my mind. Something negative about feeling a personal attraction toward him. Suddenly it hit me. He was the same size, same coloring, and similar features to men I saw frequently. This guy looked like my brothers!

I admit that I stared at him rudely. All of a sudden, I squealed, "Chuck! You're Cousin Chuck!"

"I'm Chuck Parrish. Does that make me your cousin?"

"It sure does," I shouted as I ran over and hugged him. "Callie. I'm Callie and this is Mike. Don't you remember us?"

"Of course I remember you! I just didn't recognize you. It's been a lotta years, but your family is why I decided to come through St. Mary. I was remembering those summers my parents let me stay with your family."

I recalled those long summer days, too, but there'd be time enough to talk about that later. For now, I kissed him on the cheek and gushed, "Daddy and the others will be so glad to see you. This is Mike."

"I didn't recognize him when you came in, but after you told me who you are, I'd have known he was one of the five. How's your dad and the other brothers?"

"Fine," I said and tugged on his arm. "Bring your food and come sit with us."

Chuck picked up his bowl, and I carried his iced tea to a booth. Mike was sitting there talking on his cell phone. He looked up at us as I slid in across from him and Chuck sat beside me. "Pa and Bill are on the way over. I'm calling Frank now. He's probably with Jane."

"What about John?" Chuck asked.

"Married with two kids and living in Atlanta," Mike said.

"Who else is married?" Chuck said.

"Nobody," I said. "Everybody's been married at least once except Jim. He's in the Navy, and we don't see much of him. Bill and Frank are both engaged."

Chuck picked up my left hand and touched the ring finger. "How about you, Sweet Britches?"

"Don't call me that! I'm a grown woman now."

"You didn't like it when you were a skinny brat either."

"I never was a skinny brat. Skinny maybe, but I wasn't ever a brat."

Mike laughed just as Rizzie arrived with two heaping plates of oyster pie. "What's so funny?" she asked.

"This is my cousin Chuck," I said. "He used to spend the summers with us when we were kids. He's been calling me Sweet Britches and says I was a brat. Mike thinks that's funny."

"Sweet Britches? How young were you and what did you do to earn that nickname?" Rizzie rolled her eyes suggestively.

"It's not what you think," I said. "I was only eleven the last time I saw Chuck, and he's Frank's age, so what were you, Chuck? About thirteen?"

"Yep. Then my daddy died and my mother never sent me back for the summer after that. She remarried and we settled in Florida." He'd finished eating and leaned back with his arm across the back of the seat. "I called Callie

Sweet Britches because one day she dropped a jug of honey on the floor. She slipped and sat right down in it. When she tried to push herself up, she got honey all over her hands. She was a sticky mess with honey dripping off her behind."

"I wouldn't have dropped the jar if you hadn't startled me," I protested.

"But it was so much fun watching you jump and squeal anytime we surprised you," Mike said. He'd been guilty of jumping out at me when we were little, too.

"Talkin' about sticky," Chuck said. "Remember the Fourth of July that we set that old tire on fire to use to light fireworks. We stomped in it and got burning pieces stuck to our shoes. Then ran around hollering until your dad sprayed us all with the hose. He had to buy us new shoes, and everybody got spanked but Callie."

"Yeah," Mike said and grinned. "Remember when that other cousin from Tennessee came for the weekend with his parents and we took him down in the cornfield and got him lost?"

Rizzie frowned a fake grimace. "Sounds like y'all had some really fine times," she said.

"Oh, it was fun," I said just as Daddy and Bill came in and pulled two chairs over to the booth.

"So this is Chuck, all growed up." Daddy said and shook my cousin's hand. "You look a whole lot like my brother did at your age. I've wondered how you turned out. And your mother? How is she?"

"Mom's fine. Remarried and had a couple more kids after Dad got killed in that wreck. I used to beg her to let me come back up here, but her new husband was jealous of my dad even with him dead, so we never had anything more to do with any of the Parrish family. My step-father wanted to change my last name, but I was old enough not to let that happen."

"Well, we're glad to see you now, and I hope you're gonna stay with us a while. Plenty of room for you right back in the same house you spent your summers in."

"I've got to get my car to Charleston tomorrow morning for the classic competition, but I could spend the night if it'd be all right."

"No problem." Daddy looked at my plate. "Is that oyster pie you're eating? Rizzie, do you have any more of that? I'd like a plate."

"Me, too," Bill said.

"How about you?" Daddy asked Chuck. "Want some dessert? Rizzie makes the best sweet potato pie in the world."

"Sure," Chuck answered. "I'll have a slice."

"John made me a grandpa, but these other younguns don't stay married long enough. Maybe Bill here or Frank will see to that this time around. How about you, Chuck? Got a wife and kids back in Florida?"

"Nope, not been married yet."

"Better get started before you get too old."

"Daddy!" I said, "He's only Frank's age."

"Besides," Chuck grinned. "It's not the years on the calendar. It's the miles left on the motor."

"Speaking of motors, what kind of engine you got in that Corvette?" Mike asked.

"I put an LT-1 in it, but I don't race it, just show it. I've got a few vehicles home in Florida that you'd like, too." The conversation turned to nothing but cars. If I were the kind of gal who talks that way, I would have made a comment about men and their toys.

Frank and Jane arrived and sat at the table across from our booth. They ordered shrimp po-boys. The Boys had changed the subject to reminiscing about troubles they'd gotten into as kids.

Jane seemed strangely quiet. She was wearing one of

her hippie dresses in shades of lavender and purple with purple-lensed sunglasses. Purple was one of Jane's best colors with her bright red hair, and I can honestly say that if even the barest smile had caressed her lips, she would have looked beautiful. There were no smiles. She sat silently picking the shrimp from her sandwich and eating each piece individually with her fingers instead of eating the sandwich like she normally did.

"Everybody come on over to the house," Daddy said when everyone had finished eating and paid up.

"Not me," Jane said. "I'm not feeling very well. I want to go home."

Frank patted her on the shoulder. "Come on, Jane. Get over it. Let's go to Pa's and visit with Cousin Chuck. We haven't seen him in years."

Then Jane did something she'd never done before in all the years I'd known her. She commented on her blindness. She puffed out her chest, which is naturally well-rounded anyway, and said, "I've never seen him at all."

# Chapter Twenty

"Come on," Daddy called as Cousin Chuck rolled around on the couch the next morning. "I gotcha a good country breakfast here—sausage, eggs, grits, and biscuits."

"Aghhhhh," Chuck gagged and ran to the bathroom.

The night before, I'd told Chuck that Donnie, my ex-husband, used to take my Mustang to car shows, but my cousin was more interested in picking guitars and singing with Daddy and The Boys. I picked banjo with them for a while, but Frank came in after he'd dropped Jane off at her place. He wanted to play banjo, and mine was at my apartment, so I forfeited the house instrument to him, curled up on a chair, and sang along.

The beer ran out just before midnight—not that I'd had any. It's easier to drink Diet Coke than argue with Daddy that at thirty-three, I'm old enough to have a beer. After Dad brought out the jars of Pink Stuff he kept in the back of his bedroom closet, nobody did much talking that made any sense, so I went to bed in my old room.

My daddy got drunk when I was born. I don't blame him for that. My mama died giving me life, but Daddy was still inebriated the next day when he named me. He already had five sons, but no girls before me (or after me, for that matter). He couldn't think of anything feminine except the color pink, and the only pink thing he thought of was Calamine Lotion. Thank heaven most folks call me

Callie.

When Daddy brought out the jars of Pink Stuff last night, it occurred to me to be glad he hadn't thought of it when he told the nurse what to put on my birth certificate. Being named Calamine Lotion was embarrassing enough, but Pink Stuff or Moonshine would have been worse even though Moonshine had a kinda nice '60's hippie sound. Pink Stuff *is* moonshine. Technically, Daddy's shine isn't white lightning because it's tinted pink with cherry juice.

Now morning had come and Chuck looked like he needed a little juice to pink up his complexion. He was white as a ghost, or maybe white as white lightning, which I'd never seen, when he came out of the restroom.

"Callie," Chuck said. "Did you ever go to car shows with that husband of yours?"

"I told you last night that he showed the Mustang, but I didn't go."

"How would you like to go to Charleston with me for this show? It's a big one."

"How long will it last?" Daddy asked. "Calamine's a single woman, and you're kin, but it ain't proper for the two of you to go off spending the night out of town."

Before I could remind him that I'm grown, Chuck said, "I'll treat her like my own sister." He shook his head no to the cup of coffee Daddy offered and turned to me.

"I'm assuming you'd be willing to help me drive up there," he said.

"Help you drive? It's only a couple of hours from here."

"I'm also assuming you feel better this morning than I do. I'm hoping I can get a few more hours' sleep and be up to snuff when we get there. This show's pretty important to me." He paused with a sick look on his face, then added, "That is, if you can drive an SUV pulling a trailer."

Daddy laughed. Loud. "That gal could drive a combine when she was twelve. She can drive anything that's got gas in it."

"Good." Chuck gagged again and seemed to swallow. Yuck! If anything travels from my stomach to my mouth, it goes out, not back down.

I reached for the cordless telephone. "I'll call one of my bosses and see if I can have the day off." I pressed in a number, but it wasn't for Middleton's Mortuary. "I need to call Jane, too," I explained. "She wasn't feeling well last night. That's why Frankie dropped her off before he came over. What time did he go home anyway?"

"He didn't," Daddy said. "He's asleep on the floor in Bill's room."

"How many supervisors do you have?" Chuck asked, ignoring the conversation about Jane and Frankie.

"Two, and buh-leeve me, Otis and Odell are *bosses*."

Daddy laughed and set a plate of food at my table place. I sat down and began eating while I dialed Jane. She answered with, "What in the Sam Hill are you calling me for so early in the morning?"

"Since Roxanne has slowed down her work, I figured you'd be up."

"I've been up for hours—throwing up."

"Jane! That sounds like morning sickness. Do you have something to tell me?" I grinned and scooped up a fork full of scrambled eggs.

"Nope. I think it's stress. I don't have any other signs of pregnancy. In fact, right now I'm having the major sign that I'm not."

"Some women's cycles don't stop. There are other signs. Are your nippies red?" Dad was listening. Now he grinned.

"Not to be rude, Miss Kindergarten Cussing, but how the devil would I know?"

"I guess you could ask my brother."

"He'd have to have a good memory because I don't know if I'll let him be looking again anytime soon."

"Whoa! Are you and Frankie having bigger problems?" The sausage was homemade with onions—delicious. It had been too long since I'd had breakfast at my Daddy's table.

"Let's not go there right now. Why'd you call?"

"Just to check on you and let you know I'm gonna ride to Charleston with Chuck if Otis and Odell will let me take today off. Tomorrow's my day off anyway."

"I want to go."

"I thought you were busy throwing up."

"The nausea has finally calmed down some. I'd love to get out of town. Do you think your cousin will take us by Victoria's Secret?"

"I can't make any promises, but I'll ask him. I've gotta check first with Otis and Odell to see if I can take off. I'll call you back."


Heading up Highway 17 just below the speed limit, I pretended the Suburban and Corvette on its open trailer were mine. Other drivers smiled and waved at me. They may have believed I was the owner instead of just a cousin. I was in my own proud world while Chuck and Jane nattered on, distracting me from the joy of driving this rig.

"I didn't wake Frankie up before I left Daddy's," I said and turned toward Jane, who sat in the back seat.

"Watch the road," she snapped at me.

"How does she know you're not looking at the road?" Chuck asked.

"I know because Callie *always* faces me when she's talking. Plus I can tell from her voice if she's facing me or not."

"*Cooooooool!*" Chuck said, like some leftover from another decade.

"Did you call Frankie?" I asked Jane.

"No. In case you haven't noticed, Frank and I aren't getting along as well as we were."

"I don't guess it matters that much whether you called him since he left you home alone and came over to Dad's last night. I didn't know you were sick, and I didn't know he'd stayed 'til this morning."

"That wasn't because he was mad at me. He just wanted to jam with you guys and spend time with Chuck, and I'm not one of those women who sit up at night waiting to see what time their man wanders in." She sniffled, felt around in her purse for a tissue, found it, and wiped her nose. I couldn't tell if she was about to cry or her allergies were bothering her. Had Frank been staying out some nights and Jane was too proud to admit it?

"I left a message on our land line this morning that I'd gone to Charleston with you and he'd find his lunch in the fridge."

"How'd you do that?" Chuck said.

"Called the house phone on my cell. We do that all the time since I don't write notes."

"Oh, my heaven!" I said, "That reminds me I left my cell phone at Dad's." My attention turned back to Jane. "What'd you leave him for lunch?" I asked."

"Pork chops, mashed potatoes, and lemon bars."

"He'll be a happy man!" I laughed.

"Jane cooks?" Chuck asked in a surprised tone.

"She's an excellent cook!" I confirmed.

"I just never thought about a blind person cooking," Chuck said as he reached out and tuned the radio to a country station.

"You'd be surprised at what Jane can do even though she doesn't see," I said, but no one answered me. Chuck snuggled over against the door, and Jane unlocked her seat belt and stretched out across the back seat. Soon both of them were snoring.

Ignoring the throaty, nasal serenade from Cousin Chuck beside me and Jane in the back seat was easier than sharing the beautiful morning with them would have been. Sometimes I like to just drive my Mustang for pleasure. Driving this rig with that smashing Corvette behind me was great!

The GPS led me directly to the expo center with big signs directing cars to different gates. I pulled over behind a fine-looking '57 Chevy Impala on a trailer being pulled by a bright new Escalade, reached over, and tapped Cousin Chuck's shoulder. He moaned and squeezed his eyes firmly closed. I tapped harder. He squenched even tighter. He looked so much like my brothers that I did what I would've done if he'd been John, Bill, Jim, Mike, or Frankie. I slugged him hard on his arm. That woke him.

"Hunh? Hunh?" He jumped up, knocking his head against the roof of the SUV, looking and sounding just as ridiculous as one of my brothers.

"We're here. I don't know what to do. The gates are labeled by parking lots. Which one do we use?" I asked.

"No parking lot. We're at the wrong gate. We go to the exhibitors' entrance." He blinked his eyes and shook his shoulders. "Just put it in park and let me come around. I'll drive from here." He got out of the SUV and walked around to the driver's side. Kin or not, that man had one fine looking tush. I wished Jane could see it as I scooted over to where Chuck had been sitting. Jane continued snoring, but, of course, she couldn't have seen it even if she'd been awake.

"Do you need to put Jane and me out to buy tickets or something?" I asked. "Where should we meet you?"

"You don't meet me. Just stay with me. You'll go in

as my crew, so you don't need tickets."

"You're taking a blind woman in as crew?"

"Well, I figure if she can cook and do all that stuff, she can be part of my crew."

Chuck drove away from the clustered signs and pulled up to an entrance labeled "Car Showers Only." I laughed. I knew they meant for "those who are showing cars," but I pictured cars taking showers like drivers at a truck stop. This indoor show was at the biggest, newest center in Charleston. Why couldn't the sign say, "Exhibitors Only?" Sometimes I'm almost ashamed of the South, but the show was probably being sponsored by a Yankee, so maybe the mistake wasn't a southern one.

Jane slept through Chuck showing his pre-registration papers to the man at the gate and accepting a large envelope in return. We were directed to unload the 'Vette, park the SUV, and take the show car into the expo center to its assigned parking spot—G5. Jane mumbled and grumbled, but woke up when Chuck had the car unloaded. He even took the glass out of the T-tops.

Jane and I sat in the Corvette until Chuck came back from parking the SUV. Since the car was a two-seater, Jane had to sit on my lap riding into the display area. Being her usual shy self, Jane hoisted her hiney up on my shoulder and poked her head and arm through the T-top. We entered the expo center with Jane waving her mobility cane like a movie star in a parade. Chuck handled the car like it was a part of him. He backed it in perfectly. It was a great beginning. We even had a good spot by my criteria. Near one of the snack stands and fairly close to a women's restroom.

# Chapter Twenty-One

The car looked perfect to me, but Chuck kept polishing it—inside and out, over and over. I asked why he hadn't put a tarp over it to ride up here. "If I had an enclosed trailer, I'd use a cover, but on an open trailer the wind would whip it and damage the paint."

That made sense, so I offered to help with the cleaning, but he insisted he preferred to do it himself. Jane and I finally went for something to drink. Turned out to be more of a coffee shop than I'd expected. I got a delicious Tira Misu latte and an almond biscotti.

The cute, dark-haired young man behind the counter said, "Our biscotti are made by a lady who lives near Beaufort." I don't know if he lied or not, but it was yummy.

Jane ordered chai. She'd been excited and happy as we entered the expo center, but recently, her moods changed rapidly. Now she sounded grumpy, and since I hadn't read the chalkboard menu to her, I figured she asked for chai expecting the young man to tell her they didn't have any. When Jane's in an ornery mood, she does things like that. We were both surprised when he turned away for a few minutes, then placed the steaming cup of tea in front of her. The fragrance was high quality chai.

As we stood sipping the hot beverages, Jane said, "Tell."

Jane and I have been friends long enough that we sometimes talk in short-hand. "Tell" means we're somewhere she's never been before and she wants a description of her surroundings. "This is the largest expo center I've ever been in," I said, then added, "for any kind of show. It's huge and there are cars parked in concentric circles all around. Some of them might not be operable because instead of driving them in, their owners are pushing them into position, or maybe they just don't want to crank the cars and add to the mileage. All I know is what I see. Donnie used to go to car shows, but I never went with him."

"Donnie the doctor?" Jane asked, referring to a guy I date sometimes.

"No, you know I call *him* Dr. Donald. Donnie, my ex, who, by the way, should be a cardiologist now."

"What did he show?"

"My Mustang."

"I always feel like we're showing off when we're in that car."

"You always show off in any car," I answered, thinking of Jane's wild outfits and sometimes erratic actions like waving at people with her feet when the top's down on my convertible.

"Do you see any cars like yours in here?" Jane asked and actually turned her head as though she could see.

"No, but later we'll take a walk and see if we find any Mustangs. This show isn't just Corvettes. There are lots of different kinds of cars."

"Are we in a good spot?"

"I think so. Chuck is on the outer perimeter, and, yes, we're near a ladies' room."

"I swear, Callie, sometimes I think you read me like a book." She held her cane out with her right arm, but the angle meant she didn't intend to use it. She wanted me to guide her by the elbow and lead her to the facilities.

When we came out, Jane and I stopped back at the coffee shop and each got more to drink. Can't say we got refills because we'd discarded our original cups before going to the restroom. I just *hate* seeing people carry food or drink to restrooms. I watched Chuck and other owners setting up their cars. Talk about old ladies being per-snickety, they don't hold a candle to a bunch of picky men making sure their vehicles are positioned precisely, impeccably clean, and identified by signs carefully slipped into metal holders on stands beside each chalked off parking space.

The signs intrigued me, so Jane and I walked back over to Chuck.

"Don't get near the car with those cups," he said immediately.

"We're not going to spill anything," Jane snapped back. "Do you want a coffee or some hot tea?"

"No, I'll get something when I finish here." Chuck's tone softened.

"Did you bring the sign with you or was it in the registration packet?" I asked.

"This particular show sends a placard with registration papers. I printed mine on my computer, but some people just fill 'em in with felt-tip markers."

The sign identified the owner of the car, the make, model, and other specifics with a few lines at the bottom for "comments."

Chuck identified himself as Charles Parrish, Orlando, Florida, owner of the 1976 Corvette with a custom paint job. I didn't bother to read any more of the details.

"Do you want to walk around and look at other cars?" I asked Chuck.

"Not yet," he answered. "I won't leave here until entries are parked on both sides." He glanced at the empty spaces on each side of him. "Don't want to risk some idiot scraping my baby backing into place." He used the cloth in his hand to wipe a spot on the car. It looked perfect to me.

"I think Jane and I'll take a stroll," I said. Chuck cautioned me to remember or write down our space number, G-5, so we could find our way back. I swear sometimes I think men believe women are stupid, though my personal attitude is exactly the reverse.

Cars, crowds of people, and sales booths with food or auto magazines and parts. I described everything to Jane including the good-looking men as well as the funny-looking ones.

When we returned, there were Corvettes parked on either side of G-5, but Chuck wasn't anywhere nearby. The car parked on the passenger side of Chuck's was metallic red. The sign caught my eye. When I taught kindergarten, I sometimes used Sunday's colorful comics from the newspaper as background for bulletin boards. I got the idea from magazines that suggested using comics or newspapers for gift wrapping. The sign for the red 'Vette had crimson letters and had been matted onto black and white newsprint.

Not to be rude, but I "parked" Jane near the car out of the way of the crowds and maneuvered myself into position smack in front of that sign. I bent slightly forward to read it and . . .

"*Dalmation!*" I shrieked and slapped my behind where someone had just pinched my bottom!

Jane whipped out her cane and began waving it back and forth as she tried to move through the people and get to me. At the same time, she yelled my name, "Callie! Callie! What's wrong?"

I turned around and found myself staring at a tie tack exactly like one I bought several years ago. It was a tiny silver Rod of Asclepius. Until I bought that little piece of jewelry, I'd always called the rod with a snake coiled around it a Caduceus, but the clerk had told me both the Caduceus and the Rod of Asclepius have been used as medical symbols. Since the tie tack I chose was a staff with a snake curled around it, it was a Rod of Asclepius. The Caduceus is a rod with two snakes coiled around it.

Now tell me how that whole memory flashed through my mind in the time it took me to look up from the silver tie tack to the face of my ex-husband! During that same short space of time, Jane parted the crowd like the red sea by slashing her mobility cane back and forth. Just as I saw that the pincher was Donnie, Jane whapped him on the shin with her stick.

Buh-leeve me, the words that spewed from my ex's mouth weren't kindergarten cussing. When he finally calmed down, Jane apologized.

"I'm *so* sorry!" she gushed over and over. "I didn't know it was *you*! I thought someone was hurting Callie."

I couldn't resist, I promise, I just didn't have the control not to say, "Oh, the days of Donnie hurting me are long gone."

"I would never hurt you again," Donnie said in a smooth voice, far more well-modulated than I remembered. He still appeared pretty much the same as when we divorced—tall and handsome with dark eyes and hair. His problem was his character and personality, not his looks. "What are you doing here? Showing the Mustang?" he asked.

"No, as a matter of fact, I'm with the gentleman showing this Corvette," I motioned toward Chuck's car.

"Nice paint job, but I prefer to have everything original." He was always a stroke-slap person. When we were married, he'd ruin every compliment with a follow-up statement like, "That's a really pretty dress, but it does make you look about ten pounds heavier."

For perhaps the millionth time in the past few years, I wondered what on earth made me ever think I was in love with this jerk. Good-looking? Yes. Worth a darn? Financially, yes. Character-wise, no!

Now I wondered if my two brothers who were engaged might someday experience the same attitude toward the women they now thought they couldn't live without. Was Jane already doubting her devotion to Frankie? Something sure seemed wrong between the two of them.

Immediately, Donnie went into a lecture about why his car was superior to Chuck's. He used lots of car words I'd heard from him before—original, authentic, restored, kit cars. I didn't pay much attention to them when we were married, and I didn't pay *any* attention to them now. I already knew that Donnie thought whatever he had was better than anybody else's anyway. Too bad he hadn't thought that about his wife when we were together.

"I noticed your sign with the newsprint background like my old bulletin boards," I interrupted the car lecture.

"Isn't that clever? The newspaper is actually from 1980, the year of my Corvette. I lucked up on the paper at an antique mall and decided to use it behind my signs.

"You? In an antique mall?" I couldn't help gasping.

"Well, it happens a beautiful young girl invited me to go there with her."

Like that was going to make me jealous!

"Girl?" I glared at him. "Don't you think you're old enough to date *women* now?"

"You know perfectly well that I refer to any lady under forty as a girl. In my book, you're still a girl."

"Well, frankly, I don't want to be anywhere in *your book.*"

I realized my voice was rising as Jane tugged on my sleeve.

"Callie, Callie, I need to pee."

My face turned red. Yes, I'd been married to the man. Yes, I'd slept with him. But did Jane *have* to say "pee"?

"Okay," I said, "I'll take you."

"*Now!*" Jane insisted.

I can't deny that I almost jerked her away, which is not something I normally do. Okay, so she didn't say, 'I need to be excused,' as I'd taught my kindergarten students, but my anger was really at Donnie, not Jane. I guess some of the irritation was also at myself for letting him get under my skin.

We were barely into the restroom before Jane pulled me over close to her face and whispered, "I don't really have to go. I can tell you're letting him get to you, and he's not worth it. Let's go stand by Chuck or go for another walk."

"Can't stand by Chuck. He's not by his car. I don't know where he is." I paused.

"Besides, I wanted to read Donnie's sign," I added.

"It's not worth it. You should see the way he's looking at you."

"What?" I almost screamed the word. "How do you know how he's *looking* at me?"

"I can hear it in his voice. He's the big, bad wolf, and you're the innocent little lamb. You hang around him long enough, the little lamb is going to get slaughtered."

"He just makes me so mad." I guided Jane to a stall and stepped into the one beside it. No point in wasting the opportunity. As we washed our hands afterward, I agreed with her. "Okay, when we go out, we'll go straight to Chuck's spot, and if Donnie follows, we'll just walk off into the crowd."

"Or shoot him!" Jane said, but we couldn't do that. We didn't have a gun.

# Chapter Twenty-Two

Forget about hanging out with Chuck to escape Donnie. The two of them were standing by the red 'Vette, heads together over the engine, under the hood, engaged in animated conversation. Chuck had changed clothes. He wore white slacks with a shirt imprinted with an American flag. Now I understood Donnie's red necktie. Apparently, some drivers and owners dressed to coordinate with their cars.

Chuck looked up and winked at me. "Hi, Callie, Dr. Kelly here tells me you two know each other—well."

I laughed. Jane guffawed like a hyena.

"So you've met my ex-husband. I thought you two were talking cars over there, not gossiping about me."

Chuck smirked. "So, do you go by the name Callie Kelly?"

"No! I went back to my maiden name when we divorced. Being called Callie Kelly was almost as bad as being named Calamine Lotion."

"I resent that!" Donnie snapped, but playfully.

"When the doctor came over and started questioning me about you, I thought he was quizzing me so he could hit on you," Chuck said as he winked again. "He didn't tell me he was your ex until after I'd told him that we're in a permanent relationship."

The winks made sense. Chuck had led Donnie to

believe our relationship was dating rather than kinship.

I moved closer and put my arm around Chuck. "Well, darling," I said with enough sugar in my voice to sweeten a pitcher of iced tea, "I'm sure that Donnie has his own ladies now."

"He sure didn't have any trouble getting ladies when you were married," Jane interrupted, then added, "not that I'm sure they were all ladies."

"Let's not go there," Donnie replied.

"What time's the judging?" I asked, but no one answered. They were back under the hood talking about car engines. Chuck's cell phone sounded a country song. He stepped back and answered it. I started reading Donnie's sign again aloud to Jane. The information was printed on a sheet that was posted against the newspaper background. It made a big deal out of his profession. Owner was shown as "Dr. Donald Gregory Kelly, M.D., Cardiologist, Columbia, S.C."

"Does it say, 'Accepting new patients'?" Jane asked.

"No," I answered, but before I could continue, Chuck rushed over and grabbed me. He hugged me tightly, and he stuttered. When we were children, I hurled if I was upset and scared; Chuck stuttered.

"C-C-Callie, somebody named Odell wants to t-t-talk to you." He handed me his phone.

"Callie, this is Odell," he growled in that gravely voice, like I wouldn't recognize him." He paused. "I've got some bad news."

"Who's dead?" I figured he was going to tell me to get back to St. Mary.

"What?" Jane squealed.

"Nobody's dead," Odell said. "Your father and brother are in the hospital. I think you need to be there."

"Which brother? What happened?" I asked, thinking some kind of accident.

"Frank."

I repeated the name, and Jane broke into wild screaming. "No, no, not Frankie!"

"We've been trying to call you, but you must have forgotten your cell again." I made no reply. "Bill had your cousin's number. I'm here in Charlestown at the main entrance of the expo center. Come on out and I'll take you to the hospital in Beaufort."

"But what happened?" I barely had breath enough to speak.

"Frank went to Jane's apartment to pick up something. Your father had a heart attack when he went by there and found Frank collapsed on the floor. The doctors think Frank might have been poisoned. Get on out here. We need to hurry!"

The word "confusion" doesn't do justice to the scene that followed. When I explained what had happened, Jane continued even louder screams and moans. Chuck offered to take me back to St. Mary, but I explained that Odell was here in Charleston, waiting for us. Donnie said nothing.

We were trying to figure out the direction to the "main" entrance when Chuck waved down a security guard in a golf cart. He agreed to take Jane and me. He didn't exceed any speed limits, but I was sure it was faster than walking or running. Besides, the rent-a-cop knew the way. I looked down at Jane's hand. She was holding Donnie's car sign and the newspaper matting.

"How'd you get that?" I asked.

"You tried to read it and never got to, so I brought it for you," she managed to say between her sobs. "How could Frankie have been poisoned?" she questioned without giving me a chance to scold her for taking the sign. I folded the papers and put them in my pocket, but I didn't say anything.

I didn't have any answers.

There was no problem locating Odell at the main entrance. He was parked smack at the door—in our newest hearse, a 2009 Cadillac he'd bought from a Charleston funeral home that folded. I sat in the front seat, the only seat. At least it was wide enough that Jane didn't have to sit on my lap. We sat scrunched together with her between Odell and me.

Even as distressed as she was about Frankie, Jane was as upset about riding in the hearse as she'd been when she'd ridden with me to bring a body to Charleston.

"Is there a dead person in here?" she asked.

"No, I've already dropped off the John Doe for his second post mortem," Odell said. "I was on my way to Charleston when Otis called to tell me what happened."

"What *did* happen?" I asked, hoping Jane would hush and listen.

"Frank went back to the apartment this morning after Jane left with you and Chuck. Your father was supposed to pick him up later to buy parts for some truck they're rebuilding. When your dad got there, he couldn't get Frank to come to the door, so he broke the door open. When he found Frank unconscious on the floor with vomit around him, Mr. Parrish called 911. Frank went into convulsions right as the paramedics arrived, your father had a heart attack. Paramedics carried both of 'em to the hospital. So far, it looks like Frank's ingested some kind of poison. They're running tests now to identify what kind."

"Poison!" Jane howled. "Why on earth could anyone *poison* Frankie?" She sobbed a few more minutes. "I know we haven't been getting along so well, but he'd never commit suicide." She sobbed, then added, "Would he, Callie"

"I don't think so," I answered, then turned back to Odell. "What kind of poison do they suspect? Is it something he could have gotten from farm chemicals? Daddy's always been really careful about pesticides and stuff like that."

"They don't know yet, but the doctors say he has signs of poisoning," Odell answered.

"What signs?"

"Throwing up, difficulty breathing, low blood pressure, convulsions—those symptoms point to poisoning. I'm just telling you and Callie what Bill said the doctors told him. John's on the way from Atlanta, too."

A conversation with Odell was difficult with Jane sobbing and crying out, "Oh, no. Please, God, don't let anything happen to Frankie!"

My prayers were silent and included Daddy as well as Frankie. I remembered to add a word for Otis.

When Jane finally quieted, I asked Odell, "Who'd you bring for an autopsy?"

"I told you. The John Doe, the one you found in the car outside the bookstore. They're doing further testing and gonna have some special FBI medical examiner repeat the post mortem."

"The sheriff told me they think they know who he is. I was supposed to call, but I was too upset when I left the shower."

"I heard the party kind of got out of hand," Odell growled.

"Is it okay if I call him now?" I asked, not wanting to tell my boss that the shower wasn't what upset me the most. It was the cow patty I'd stepped in on the way back to my car.

"Sure. You can probably hear now." Jane had settled down to just sniffling.

"I mean may I use your phone. You were right. I forgot mine again."

Odell handed me his cell, and I started to punch in

the number. He stopped me. "The sheriff is on speed dial," Odell said.

"Sheriff Wayne Harmon," he answered.

"This is Callie. You said call you and you'd tell me about the man in the Jaguar," I said.

"We're not sure, but we've learned that our Jaguar man never played golf with Mr. Johnson, or Joyner if you prefer. They didn't associate often and were seldom seen with one another, but one employee remembers seeing them together occasionally. He said they were usually riding together in a golf cart, but not playing."

"That would be a good place to talk without worrying about people hearing you," I said.

"Yes, and it makes us wonder if they had secret business together. Maybe they were old friends, really old friends, from back in the eighties."

I could almost feel the spark in my brain. "Do you think Jaguar John Doe may have been involved with Johnny Johnson's armored car heist?"

"That's exactly what I think, and I want you to help me by talking more to the Joyner woman. Maybe see if she's holding out on us."

"When will you let her bury Mr. Joyner?" I asked.

"Georgette thinks holding off will encourage her to talk more. Mrs. Joyner is very eager to get that man in the ground."

"Who?"

"Agent Georgette Randolph with the FBI."

Suddenly, I realized that Harmon hadn't said a word about my father or brother. "You do know about Frankie and Daddy, don't you?" I asked.

"What about them?"

"They're in the hospital. The doctors think Frankie's been poisoned, and Daddy had a heart attack when he found him."

The sheriff's words went above college level cussing. "I've had a call that there is a suspected poison case at the hospital, but no one said it was a Parrish."

"I'm headed there now with Odell."

"I'll see you there."

The rest of the ride took forever.

# Chapter Twenty-Three

Where to go first? Whose bedside? My daddy could be in a life-or-death situation. My brother could be dying from poison. Neither Odell nor I knew if Otis's improvement continued or may have had a setback while Odell went to Charleston.

I wasn't trying to be selfish or rude. I promise I wasn't, but I asked Odell to take Jane, and I struck off by myself at the hospital entrance while they went to park the hearse in the truck area.

The dilemma was solved by the other Donnie in my life, Dr. Donald Walters.

"Callie," he called when he saw me. His step quickened as he approached. "Good news," he continued. "Your dad is doing much better. He *did* have a mild heart attack, but the cardiologist expects a full recovery. He'll probably be moved to a regular room tomorrow."

"Where is he? Where's my brother?"

"Your dad's in the Coronary Intensive Care Unit and your brother's in Medical Intensive Care."

"Is that where Otis is?"

"No, it's where Otis *was*. He's already been moved to a regular room."

"That means he's better?" I'd forgotten how fast Donald walked. I almost had to run to keep up with him.

"Otis is definitely better."

"Have you seen Sheriff Harmon?" I asked.

"Yes, he's in your brother's room while Bill and Mike wait to see your father. Mr. Parrish has been given some sedation but he's still very upset about your brother, and he's asked for you and John. He needs to see that you're here, and the nurses are going to let you in when you arrive, but you can only stay a few minutes."

"Then I should see Daddy first?"

"Absolutely your father. The procedure they've started on Frank has him sleeping. He's not going to know if you're there are not. Let your dad see you." He paused. "I'll lead you."

We passed through the Coronary Intensive Care waiting room. Bill and Mike jumped up and hurried to Donald and me. "We've seen him," Bill said, "but he's asking for you. Says he shouldn't have let you go to Charleston."

"Come on," Donald said, "I'll take you in just in case the nurses try to give you any trouble about visiting times."

My daddy has always been the strongest person in my life. I'd never seen him in the hospital before, hardly ever even seen him sick with a cold. When Donald led me past the nurses' desk to the bed, Daddy looked old and weak. There were machines on each side of him with tubes and wires running to his body. My heart lurched in my chest. His eyes were closed, but they popped open when I stood by his side.

"Calamine?" His voice sounded hoarse and feeble.

"It's me, Daddy," I said and reached over to hold his hand. I couldn't take my eyes off the machines with their graphs tracing hills and valleys on the paper. The patterns looked regular to me, but I'm not familiar enough with them to interpret whether they were good or bad.

"Calamine?" Daddy said again.

"Yes, Daddy, I'm here and John's on the way."

"How's Frank?"

"He's doing well, Mr. Parrish," Donald answered before I had a chance to confess that I didn't know. "Your doctor wants you to rest, so Callie's going to wait with her brothers. You try to sleep and perhaps when you wake up, your son John will be here."

Daddy's lips curved into something that was almost a smile, and he closed his eyes. Donald led me back to the waiting room. He assured Bill and Mike that Daddy was doing as well as expected and explained that he was going to take me to see Frank.

"We'll go with you," Mike said.

"Even with a doctor, they aren't going to let three of you in at a time. You know the rules are no more than two visitors." Donald's voice had gone from friend to doctor.

"I'll wait outside then. Just want to know how he's doing." Bill said.

When the four of us reached Medical Intensive Care, Donald had us all sit in that waiting room while he went in to clear bringing visitors in when it wasn't visiting time, which was no more than two visitors at a time, for no more than a total of ten minutes, only on even hours.

The first thing I saw when Donald led me to my brother's bedside was Sheriff Wayne Harmon in the corner of the tiny room. Wayne was my older brother John's best friend all through high school and probably felt that the younger boys were like brothers to him. I know he'd always treated me like a little sister.

"Hi, Callie," he whispered. "The doctors haven't learned what kind it was, but all the signs are that Frank's ingested poison. The good news is that he's responding to the treatment."

I stepped closer to the bed and touched Frankie's fingertips. IV lines ran from both hands to bags hanging on poles beside the bed. Another line ran into his neck. "Frankie?" I whispered. There was no response. "Frankie?" Just a bit louder.

"Honey, he's knocked out too deeply to hear you," Donald said, and though I wanted my brother to know I was there, I was pleased that Donald had called me "Honey." Maybe he was still interested. Not that I had any intention of a serious relationship with Dr. Donald Walters. I knew from the past that he was a player, but my recent dating life had been nonexistent. Then I scolded myself mentally for thinking about romance at such a critical time.

"Can Bill and Mike come in?" I asked.

"I'll bring them, but only for a moment." Donald reached for my hand and led me back to the waiting room.

I heard her before I saw her.

Jane wailed, "Oh, Frankie, my Frankie." She and Odell stepped off the elevator with Jane whacking her mobility cane back and forth and pulling away from Odell as though she could find her way around this strange place without guidance.

"Hush, Jane!" I said in a tone much harsher than I should have. "Frankie's asleep and the other sick people here don't need to hear you howling like that."

Odell gently pushed Jane toward me and said, "You take her." I touched Jane on the arm, and Odell stepped back into the elevator and closed the doors.

"If you get quiet and be patient, Dr. Donald will let you see Frankie," I told Jane.

We both knew that her "seeing" Frankie meant to be in his presence and touch him.

One by one, Jane, Bill, and Mike went to see Frankie. I thought I should go with them when Dr. Donald escorted Jane in, but he told me she'd probably be better without me. The sheriff didn't come out with any of them.

I wondered if he was that upset. Did he know something that Donald wasn't telling us?

"Okay, now you people need to decide which waiting room you're going to sit in and let the nurses take care of your father and brother until the next visiting hour," Dr. Donald told us as we all settled back in the Medical ICU waiting room.

"I think we should split up," I said. "Some of us wait here and the rest at Coronary. Just in case there's a change in either of them. They'll come out and tell us, won't they?" I turned toward Donald.

"I'm staying here near Frank," Jane insisted before Donald could answer.

"Yes, the staff will try to keep you posted on any changes, and I'll check on both of them as often as I can. I've got to go now. It's time for me to make rounds. I'll see all of you later." He walked away.

Bill and Mike decided to wait for John in the Coronary ICU waiting room and leave Jane and me here outside Frankie's unit. As they stepped onto the elevator, a Jade County uniformed deputy stepped out. Fast Eddie Blake! What in tarnation was *he* doing here?

I don't know, I *promise* I don't know if it was intentional or not, but Mike and Deputy Blake bumped into each other. Not hard. Not much. Just a little bump!

"Watch it!" Blake snapped.

"Watch it yourself!" Mike answered in the same tone. "Whatcha going to do? Put me in jail for accidentally bumping into an . . ." I won't repeat what Mike called the deputy.

"I could arrest you for assaulting an officer," Blake said. Too loud. Everyone in the area looked at him.

"I doubt it with all these witnesses," Mike sniped.

The deputy didn't get a chance to respond because Sheriff Harmon rushed through the Intensive Care doors with fire in his eyes.

"I thought I recognized the idiots who yell in hospitals where critically ill people are trying to rest and get better." His face grimaced into anger. "What's going on?"

"This deputy here arrested me Saturday night and put me in jail for no good reason at all," Mike explained.

"He bumped me. That's assaulting an officer," Blake tried to talk over him.

"If you're not lying on the floor, bleeding, or bruised, forget it!" Harmon said to Blake, then turned to Mike. "You'll have a chance to explain everything about Saturday night to the judge. Right now, you need to go down to wait with Bill." He turned toward the deputy and scowled. "You're here because I called you, Officer Blake."

"Yeah, I thought you were letting me use your fishing cabin on the lake for my days off. Now you've called me in. What am I supposed to do, Sir?"

"I'm putting a chair right outside Frank Parrish's room. You are to sit in it and make sure no one who's not authorized goes in. I've also requested that no one is to see him alone. Whenever nurses, doctors, or visitors go in, it's to be in pairs, and don't forget—no visitors except immediate family." He motioned toward Blake and said, "Come with me."

Either Mike or Bill pressed the button to close the doors to the elevator and they disappeared. Jane and I waited. When Sheriff Harmon came back, he sat beside me.

"What's going on?" I asked.

"The two surviving perps of the Buckley armored car robbery in 1980, Johnny Johnson and Noah Gordon, have died within twenty-four hours of each other, apparently murdered. Toxicology's not back, but it appears that both of them were poisoned. We don't know what kind, but we're pretty sure of that. The docs think your brother's been poisoned, too. I don't know what the connection might be, but on the chance that there's some relationship, I'm having Frank guarded until I have more answers."

"You think Frankie was poisoned intentionally?" Jane asked.

"I don't know, but I'm not taking any chances."

"But *what* kind of association could Frankie have with two old men from Hilton Head who turn out to have robbed an armored car years ago?" I said.

"I have no idea," the sheriff said, "but Frank could have seen or heard something that relates to the homicides. He may not even be aware of what it was, but it might be enough for the murderer to try to get rid of him." The sheriff glanced toward the elevator and repeated, "I'm not taking any chances." He paused. "I've gotta go now."

I grasped the sleeve of his shirt. "Isn't there *anyone* else you could assign to guard Frankie?"

"Blake came to us highly recommended. I think he has some problems adjusting to the difference in a big city police force and a small town sheriff's department, but I'm the sheriff, and I believe he's the best man for the job."

Sheriff Harmon didn't even say goodbye. He just stepped into the elevator, closed the doors, and left Jane and me sitting there in shock.

# Chapter Twenty-Four

As upset as Jane was about Frankie, she went to sleep sitting in the waiting room. I couldn't sleep, but I couldn't concentrate either. I tried reading magazines, then tried watching television, gave up and just watched the other people. Some of them slept, some cried, and others almost seemed to be in trances. A volunteer kept asking us if we'd like coffee. She was a middle-aged lady with a very pleasant manner, but the only thing I wanted was for my daddy, my brother, and my boss to all get well and go home.

I stared at the elevator doors and eventually, it paid off. My brother John showed up. He's my only openly affectionate brother and he gave me a big bear hug. "Pretty rough day, isn't it?" he asked.

"Awful," I said. "You know Otis is here, too. Had pneumonia, but he's doing better."

"What's this about Frank being poisoned? Have they told you what it was? Do they think it was an accident? I can't see Frank poisoning himself, and I don't know any reason someone would try to kill him."

"Your guess is as good as mine." I sat down and glanced at the large round clock on the wall, just like the ones on classroom walls. "It's almost time for visiting. You can go in this time. Jane and I have already been. Don't be upset by the deputy. Sheriff Harmon's being careful."

"So Wayne must think the poison might have been given to Frank intentionally."

"I guess so, but the deputy is the biggest jerk I've ever seen. Just wait 'til you meet him."

"I definitely don't look forward to that."

Jane groaned and turned her head the other way. Her mouth flopped open and I thought I should close it for her, but when I attempted to push her lower jaw up, she tried to bite me, so I decided to leave her looking stupid.

Sheriff Harmon arrived just before visiting time. He and John had been friends since childhood. While they chatted, I pretended to look at a magazine and eavesdropped. Jane and I call that "dipping," and sometimes we come up with something good. I heard John suggest various poisons to the sheriff. "Strychnine?" John said.

"Nope, strychnine is used in books because it's dramatic, but Frank's symptoms didn't include the contortions of the spine and some of the other ugliness that goes with strychnine."

"Arsenic?"

"Not likely. No point in trying to guess anyway, John. They'll let us know when it's identified. Just be glad your father found him when he did. Whatever it was, the convulsions were pretty bad. At least, he hadn't been like that long. Mr. Parrish left for the apartment not long after Frank headed there. He said Frank was fine at the house. I impounded your brother's truck. Forensics folks are going over it. I'd hoped to find something he'd eaten in the truck, but no luck there."

"What's wrong with this deputy you've got sitting with him? Callie talks like she hates him."

"There's nothing *wrong* with him. He's just over-enthusiastic. He came highly recommended, but he doesn't have that laid-back Southern attitude. I've got other personnel working on the case, too."

"Mike told me that Callie found another body outside the bookstore. What's that about?"

"There was a car parked in front of the store. Callie noticed the man in it. Turned out he was dead. An elderly man that we've just identified as an FBI most wanted from an armored car robbery in 1980. Three men shot a guard during that robbery in New Jersey. They were Johnny Johnson, Noah Gordon, and Leon McDonald. A man called Harold Joyner died in the Beaufort Hospital of a gastroenteritis infection. Turns out he's Johnny Johnson. The man your sister found appears to be the partner Noah Gordon. Both of them have been autopsied and seem to have been poisoned. Toxicology's not back yet to identify the kind or source."

"Any info on the third man?"

"The third thief was Leon McDonald. He was caught and sentenced to life for the death of the guard. Less than a year later, he was beaten to death in prison."

"Is that all you know about him?"

"He never ratted the others out. Went to his grave silent about his partners."

John looked down at his watch just as the volunteer announced, "Visitors have a total of ten minutes. No more than two persons at a time per patient."

As John and the sheriff headed for the doors, I said, "Please come out in time to let Jane and me go back there for a few minutes."


Our next visit was exactly like the one before except that Fast Eddie Blake's eyes shifted from glaring at me to staring at Jane's boobs. I guess he was ticked off to be there instead of at the lake fishing.

The days and nights after that blurred into each other.

We alternated between seeing Daddy and Frankie with a couple of detours by Otis's room. Otis improved enough to go home. His ex-wife went with him.

Getting better took longer for Daddy and Frankie. When Jane and I went home for showers during the two hours between even visitation hours, the apartment showed signs of having been searched. Sheriff Harmon confirmed that they had removed several things as possible poisons, including a can of bug spray, a gallon of antifreeze, and some cleaning supplies.

After Frankie was dismissed from the hospital, life began getting back pretty much to normal. My loved ones were out of the hospital with Frankie being cared for at the apartment by Jane and Daddy back to bossing everyone around at his house. When I called to tell Odell I'd be returning the next day, he said Otis would be coming in, too.

I climbed into the Mustang, careful not to close the door on the skirt of my black dress. Headed back to work for the first time since I returned from the car show, I almost felt happy to be going to work. FBI and local law enforcement had finally released Harry Joyner, AKA Johnny Johnson, to Mrs. Joyner for burial. When I'd talked to Odell the night before, he'd told me my morning duty would be to ride with Mrs. Joyner to Taylor's Cemetery. We were to leave the funeral home at eleven A.M. for the interment. Once again, Mrs. Joyner didn't want any gas guzzling limos nor a funeral coach. The woven basket casket was being carried to the cemetery in a fuel-efficient vehicle owned by one of Mrs. Joyner's friends.

# Chapter Twenty-Five

I didn't say anything because I *couldn't* say anything. I'd opened the door to my office and found Otis's ex-wife Darlene sitting behind my desk. That wasn't especially shocking because Denise always sits there while she catches the phone for me when I'm out. What left me speechless was that a cardboard box on the floor held all my personal things from the top of the desk as well as the drawers. Two books from the back of the bottom drawer topped the pile of my belongings. The surface of the desk had been completely rearranged.

"Otis wants to see you the minute you arrive," Darlene said in that Mae West voice.

"Where is he?" Buh-leeve me. I wanted to talk to *him*.

"He said he'd be in the prep room." She glanced down at the box, pointed, and added, "Take that with you."

"Where do you want me to put it?" I realized the minute the words escaped my mouth that I'd left myself open for a crude reply, but Darlene let that opportunity pass.

"It's all personal. You can put it in your car."

Did this mean Otis wanted to see me to fire me?

I backed out of my office, or maybe I should say Darlene's office, dragging the box with me, and headed for the prep room. Did we have a new decedent? Was

Otis feeling strong enough to do the embalming? I'd temporarily forgotten that Otis spends half his time in the prep area in his tanning bed, which is where I found him when I entered.

Otis looked surprised to see me. He pulled on a robe and said, "I didn't expect you so early. Let's sit down and talk." He looked around and seemed to realize that the prep room isn't exactly set up for conversation. "Tell you what. Get two cups of coffee and meet me in the front consulting room. I'll get dressed and see you in a few minutes."

Middleton's policy is that coffee is served in Wedgwood cups from a silver service up front, but we each have a personal mug for the back. I took the box to the front and left it on the table in the consulting room. In the kitchen, I filled two mugs with coffee. I usually put both cream and sweetener in mine, but I was in the mood to rough it. I took the coffee to the front, put the cups on the round table, sat in an overstuffed velvet chair, and waited. My stomach chose to do flips. Nausea flooded over me. When I get scared, I barf, but I wasn't fearful of Otis. Why'd I feel this way?

No, I wasn't frightened of Otis, but I *was* afraid of losing my job through no fault of my own. I felt useful working at the mortuary. I did a good service—making people look good for their loved ones, creating beautiful memories. I didn't want to go back to teaching kindergarten where I dealt with little people who wouldn't be quiet, wouldn't be still and had to tee tee every five minutes. I didn't want to go back to working in a beauty parlor where I listened to gossip and complaints about husbands all day. I wanted to keep my job at Middleton's.

"Callie," Otis called my name in his most comforting Undertaking 101 voice. "I know that finding Darlene in your office must have surprised you. She insisted on staying with me until I'm fully recovered and wants to do her old job while she's here." He motioned toward the box of my belongings. "I didn't expect her to do this."

"Are you firing me?" I've never been accused of being particularly tactful, and I wanted to know my position—if any.

"No, I'm not firing you. I'm just asking you to be patient. Dealing with Darlene was never easy, and I'm not up to it now physically or mentally. I'm back at work today to get away from her and she insisted on coming in with me. That's why I was in the prep room."

"If she gets on your nerves, why were you asking for her when you were so sick?" I took a sip of coffee and thought Darlene must have made it. The brew was strong enough to walk, or in Darlene's case, chase someone away from a job that person loved.

"I don't know. I guess when a person's really ill, having someone you used to love seems comforting." He sipped his coffee, grimaced, looked at the mugs with a questioning expression, and asked, "Where's the Wedgwood? Has someone broken some pieces?"

"Oh, no. I just thought we'd use the mugs since it's just you and me."

I never found out what Otis's answer to that was because "Just As I Am" played on the sound system. I put my mug on the table and stepped into the hall. Mrs. Joyner stood there. She wore a brown dress with rust-colored flowers printed on it and a bright orange shawl. For some reason, I expected her to have on some kind of hippy-type sandals, but she wore low-heeled brown pumps.

"Good morning, Miss Parrish," she said. "Mr. Middleton is putting Harry into my friend's minivan, so we're ready. I'm parked out front."

I hadn't seen Odell since my arrival, but since Otis

had been with me, Odell had to be the "Mr. Middleton" who was assisting with Mr. Joyner.

Happy to have an excuse not to hear a long tale about Otis's marriage to Darlene, I followed Mrs. Joyner out to her hybrid car. "Buckle up," she said the minute I'd closed the car door.

Sheriff Harmon had asked me to talk to her about her husband. "Once again," I said, "I'm so sorry for your loss."

"It was a shock. I have to confess that I'm growing used to being alone, but I'm still in shock to find out Harry wasn't really Harold Joyner. The man I knew and loved wasn't at all the person the sheriff talked about. I just can't imagine Harry being a thief. It's very hard to think about living fifteen years with a man whose whole life was a lie."

"I know it must be very hard for you." I thought about the shrink's question. *How does that make you feel,* but it didn't seem appropriate or necessary. She told me anyway.

"One of the most difficult parts is learning that Harry deserted his wife and three kids. Guess that explains why he never agreed to get married. Not that we could since he didn't have any real ID. I used to feel guilty that we met too late to have children. He liked to go to the park and watch the little ones play. I don't mean that in a dirty way, like a pedophile or something like that. I mean he seemed to really enjoy kids in a good way. Then to find out that he abandoned his own children and left them penniless when he had all that money to spend and live the rich life."

"I understand," I said. I hadn't expected her to pour out her feelings like that, and I couldn't think of anything to say. I mean what was I supposed to tell her? She had wanted him to make their union legal. I didn't believe I should inform her that I found it surprising that a man who'd rob an armored car would be too good to commit bigamy.

Her expression suddenly became extremely sad. "I even told the sheriff that if he'd make the arrangements, I'd like to send some money to Harry's wife and children."

That was an interesting thought. "What did he say?" I asked.

"He said that the money came from the robbery and wouldn't be mine to give away." She sniffled and touched her nose with a tissue from the box on the console. "Are you married?"

"No, ma'am. Divorced."

"I really enjoyed those years with Harry, but I always assumed that if something happened to him, I'd be left with enough to live on. Now it seems I won't be, and I'm not a spring chicken anymore. It might be difficult to find another wealthy man to take care of me."

I couldn't think of a thing to say. I couldn't say, "Oh, you'll be okay against the twenty-year olds," because we both knew better. Perhaps some other wealthy golfer would woo her into marriage before he found out she was broke. If not, I supposed she'd have to go back to serving crab cakes and cocktails.

Mrs. Joyner ignored my silence and smiled, "I'd almost forgotten. Sheriff Harmon told me about your father and brother being hospitalized. I'm so glad they're doing better."

"Thank you. We were right worried for a while."

"Did the sheriff tell you about the dead man you found being my Harry's partner when the robbery took place?"

"Yes, ma'am."

"And they were both poisoned, though he hasn't told me what kind yet." She paused and looked at me, obviously expecting an answer.

"I don't think the toxicology reports have identified what poison killed either of them nor what kind made my brother so sick." I was supposed to be trying to get information from Mrs. Joyner, but I felt like she was interrogating me.

When we pulled through the gates into Taylor's Cemetery, I was surprised to see Middleton's awnings over a recent grave across from where the awnings and chairs were set up for the Joyner interment. I couldn't swear they were the same people, but the vehicles and number of men and women standing around Mr. Joyner's resting place seemed about the same as when we'd planted the tree.

The late heat wave had let up just a little, and the air felt crisply autumn. The wooded area that surrounded the sides and back of the cemetery had begun to shift from green to crimsons and golds. The crape myrtle we'd planted at Mr. Joyner's first funeral had no blossoms and the limbs, though not bare, had far fewer leaves.

Mrs. Joyner parked in the same place she had before, and we got out and headed for the gravesite. Odell was standing at the head of the basket casket, which was topped with a spray of wild flowers tied with raffia.

As before, there wasn't a pastor there. Mrs. Joyner stood up and welcomed "friends." She didn't mention "family," probably because the Hilton Head Mr. Joyner had no family. I doubted she'd thought to invite the Johnson family from New Jersey.

After the service was over and everyone had spoken to Mrs. Joyner, she thanked Odell for all Middleton's had done.

"I appreciate your getting the special casket and working with me on all of this," she said. "Now I want to ask one more favor. My friends want me to head back to Hilton Head and have lunch with them. Would it be all right for Callie to ride back to St. Mary with you?"

"Certainly, Mrs. Joyner. We'll be in touch when the death certificates come. We ordered you three copies. Thank you for letting us serve you in your time of grief."

As Mrs. Joyner and her friends drove out of the cemetery, I thought, "There go the green people." That brought up an image of squat little people with big green heads, like the space aliens in those papers by the grocery store check outs. I giggled.

"What's funny?" Odell asked. He was watching the workers lower the casket and fill in the grave. It seemed strange to watch dirt fall directly onto the coffin instead of a vault or grave liner. I thought I saw the top dip in a little as the dirt hit it, but that was probably my imagination.

"Just a funny thought," I answered Odell. I pointed to the Middleton's awning across the area. "Who's that?" I asked.

"Evan Taylor. You were off when we buried him. Actually, this place started out as the Taylor family graveyard, but when times got hard, they expanded and began selling plots. Evan's buried in one of the original family plots. I think he's a cousin of some kind. Bet you're glad you didn't get stuck with sitting up all night at that wake his wife had for him. Jake said it was one long bout of drinking and eating and crying. Said that trailer was packed with people."

"I'd just as soon not have been there for that. Did he tell you that's the third husband she's held a wake for in that mobile home?"

Odell guffawed. "Yep, heard about that, too."

The men were disassembling the awning and packing the chairs into their van. "Let's go," Odell said and followed me to his Buick.

I'd waited as long as I could. "Odell," I said, "did you go along with Otis on letting Darlene take over my job?" I didn't even wait for an answer before adding another question. "And am I fired? Is she going to cosmetize as well as answer the phone and keep up with the obituaries and online information?"

"What do you mean? Darlene just came in to be with Otis on his first day back."

"It doesn't look like that. She's cleaned out my desk and packed my belongings in a box that she told me to put in my car."

"What in tarnation is Doofus doing now? Surely he's not going to marry her again."

"He didn't say anything about a wedding. He just said for me to be patient."

"Don't worry about it until I talk to Doofus. Like he said, 'Be patient.' You know patience is a virtue."

"Well, sometimes I feel like I've been too danged virtuous too danged long."

# Chapter Twenty-Six

"I need some barbecue," Odell said when he pulled up in front of the funeral home to let me out. We'd both been mostly silent on the way from Taylor's to St. Mary. The only sound had been an occasional growl from Odell's stomach and at least one rumble from mine. It was after lunch time for us.

Since my boss put me out at the front instead of the employee entrance, I was welcomed by "Amazing Grace." Darlene came rushing to the foyer.

"Sheriff Harmon wants you to call him," she told me. I kinda felt important, like she was my secretary, until she added, "and from now on, you need to check with me when you leave and let me know when you return." So much for Darlene being my secretary. Now she thought she was my boss! Then again, she acted like I was going to be around, so maybe she wasn't planning to push the Middletons to fire me after all.

I called Harmon's office expecting to be told he'd call me back, but he was on the line in a less than a minute.

"Hi Callie, have you had lunch? I'll treat you at Gastric Gullah if you'll meet me over there."

"How soon? I'm starving."

"Head there now."

"Sure." Any other time, I'd have had to ask Otis and Odell if this would be a good time for me to go to lunch, but I figured since Darlene was doing my job, I was free to take lunch whenever I pleased.

We were late enough that Rizzie's lunch crowd had thinned down. Wayne and I chose the booth in the back corner. I assumed he wanted to quiz me about any information Mrs. Joyner might have given me earlier.

"Seat yourselves," Rizzie called when she saw us. "House special today is pork cooked with red rice and there's two servings left. Y'all want that or shall I bring menus?"

"You can dip mine up right now and bring an iced tea with it," Sheriff Harmon said.

"Me, too," I called.

Harmon didn't wait long to ask, "Did Mrs. Joyner tell you anything new?"

"Not really, but you've upset her."

"How? I thought letting her bury her husband would make her happy. She sure bugged me enough about getting the body released."

Rizzie set the plates and tea in front of us.

"But you told her she can't keep the money. Now she's worried she won't find another rich husband. She'd planned on Joyner's money lasting the rest of her life."

I took a big bite of red rice. Best I'd ever tasted.

"Unfortunately, Mr. Joyner's money was actually Johnny Johnson's illegal gains. Mrs. Joyner swears he never revealed where he kept his money. She only had access to funds he put in a home safe for her use. He was generous, but he kept the big money somewhere she didn't know about."

"Do you have any new leads?"

The sheriff put his fork on the side of his plate and drank about half his glass of tea in one long gulp. "That meat's mighty succulent, but it's a bit hot for me."

I sliced off a bite of pork and tasted it. Tender, juicy, and *hot*. I finished off my tea and waved to Rizzie for more.

"No new leads, but I have several theories," the sheriff said. Rizzie refilled our glasses. Wayne and I both emptied them. She filled them again.

"Is that pork too high seasoned for you?" Rizzie asked.

"It's a bit hot," Sheriff Harmon said.

"Maum cooked it, and she seasons more than I do. If you don't like it, you can order something else, but it will hurt her feelings."

"Where is she?" I asked.

"She came in with me this morning," Rizzie said. "Since she began leaving the island, she likes to cook here. She's been hoping you'd be by today, so she can ask you about doing her nails sometime soon."

Maum is Rizzie's grandmother. She's an ancient Gullah woman who loves to have her fingernails painted bright red. I go out to Surcie Island, where she lives, and give her manicures and pedicures. I was a few weeks overdue.

"Is she still here?"

"In the kitchen. She doesn't like coming out to the dining area, but she loves that kitchen. Step on back and speak to her if you want."

I'd never been beyond the dining area, and I guess it looked like any other small restaurant's work place. Maum was scrubbing the range top though it looked immaculate to me. She grinned and gave me a gigantic hug for such a tiny lady.

"Oh, Callie. It's so good to see you." She held up her hands in front of me, then realized she was wearing yellow rubber gloves. When she tossed them on the counter, I saw her chipped nail polish.

"Well, you'll be seeing me soon, unless you want to hang around the restaurant when you get finished. I can come back and do your nails then."

"That would be wonderful. I've gotten used to seeing them lookin' pretty. I plumb hate to go to church when they look like this."

"Ask Rizzie to call me when you're off work," I said, gave her another hug, and went back to Sheriff Harmon.

"Sorry about that," I said to him. "Rizzie's Maum is a very special lady."

"That's understandable. While you were gone, I ordered two pieces of sweet potato pie."

"Sounds like a plan."

"The feds are investigating the heist and, of course, these two murders are related, but I'm still keeping a hand in the homicides. I've considered that Johnny Johnson may have either killed or paid someone to get rid of Leon McDonald. Then, if he was able to take over all the money and confessed it to his wife, Mrs. Joyner may have done him in and expected to walk away with what's left of the robbery take."

"If you can believe that, then why couldn't Mrs. Joyner have known about it all along? Maybe she and Harry were having problems. She thought he would dump her, and she poisoned both of them. After all, from what I've read, poison is usually a female method of murder."

"That's definitely a possibility."

Rizzie set two large pieces of pie on the table. The sheriff pulled his over and forked himself a huge bite. He moaned with pleasure, then looked embarrassed.

"Next time we come here," he said, "I'm skipping the entrée and just ordering a whole pie."

"That might ruin that trim waistline," I quipped.

The sheriff rubbed his washboard abs. "It would be

worth it. Wish I could find me a woman who cooks pie like this."

"Rizzie is a woman who cooks pie like that."

"She's too young for me."

"Her grandmother's in the kitchen," I teased.

As Harmon paid our bill, Rizzie told me, "Maum's finished. She said tell you she'll wait in the kitchen until you're through work. Tyrone is picking her up when I call him. She said be sure you understand she doesn't mind waiting for you.

"I'll try to be back soon. If I had the supplies in my car, I'd do her nails right now." I didn't say a word to Sheriff Harmon about Tyrone. I know for a fact that Rizzie's brother isn't old enough to have a driver's license.

In the Mustang, on the way back to the mortuary, I hoped we didn't have any new decedents. I claim that I neither give nor take guilt trips, but I was ashamed that I'd neglected Maum so long. When I'd first begun going to her house on Surcie Island to do her nails, I'd been very faithful about never letting the polish look ragged. I'd enjoyed my time with her, listened with pleasure to tales of her early years. Then I'd gotten busy and postponed a few times. It had been like going to church. If I miss a few weeks, it becomes harder and harder to make it there on the Sunday mornings I'm not working. Each time, I think, "Well, I'll go next week."

Odell met me at the employee entrance. "I've been watching for you. We need to talk," he said.

My stomach flipped around the sweet potato pie I'd eaten. Had he discussed me with Otis? Were they going to let me go?

"Here?" I asked.

"No, in my office." I followed him. He shut the door and gestured for me to sit down.

"I've got some good news and some bad news,"

Odell grumbled.

*Dalmation!* Was the good news that I could draw unemployment after the bad news dismissal?

"You know, Otis was *really* sick," he said.

"Yes."

"He's got some crazy idea that he needs Darlene to take care of him."

"Maybe he's been lonely. He doesn't go out as often as you do. He leads a pretty solitary life. Since he bought his own tanning bed, he doesn't even go to the sun parlor."

"Stop defending him. If he's lonely, he should ask some woman out for a date. Lord knows we meet enough nice widows through the business." Odell harrumphed, which he does anytime he's irritated. "Anyway, the bad news is that until Otis is over his delusion, Darlene has taken over your office. She also wants to cosmetize, which she did occasionally while she and Doofus were married. This doesn't leave a lot for you to do except computer work, and she wants you to teach her how to do that."

My back hackled. "Are you telling me to teach Darlene to do the computer so she can take my job?"

"No, I'm telling you the same thing Otis told you. Be patient. I think he just said that to pacify you. I'm saying it to let you know that you're not being fired. Otis and Darlene fought all the time when they were married. It won't take long for one of them to get angry enough to put an end to this, and things will go right back to normal."

I cannot tell a lie. Well, I can, but I didn't then. "This is all pretty disturbing to me. If we don't have any new clients, I'd like to take the afternoon off."

"That's fair, but I don't want you getting upset and looking for another job. You're the best cosmetician we've ever had." I beamed. Compliments don't come freely from Odell.

"Then could you maybe rearrange the schedule so that I'm off this Sunday?" In for a penny, in for a pound. All those thoughts about church made me think maybe I should try to attend worship services more often. I'd been trying to defend myself by saying I heard enough from preachers at funeral services, but Daddy was right when he told me that was just a cop-out.

I stopped by my work room, changed out of my black dress and into the jeans, tee, and tennis shoes I keep in my locker. I grabbed the manicure case. Technically, it belongs to Middleton's, but I frequently pick up polishes out of my own pocket when I see shades I like on sale. This time I'd let Maum choose from the many colors instead of just carrying red with me like I usually did. If Darlene needed the kit before I got back, it was just TS, which in kindergarten cussing means something bad, or tough stinky.

Surprise, surprise! Maum chose the brightest red nail polish in the collection. I'd finished her fingernails and was in the kitchen with her bare left foot propped in my lap while I worked on her calluses. Rizzie came barreling through the swinging doors announcing, "Callie, somebody wants to see you." Cousin Chuck was right behind her.

Maum jerked her foot from me and scrambled for her socks. "Rizzie, don't you let a man in here when I'm not fully dressed." I didn't know the little old lady could move so fast. She had her shoes on and laced up in a flash.

"Ma'am, I'm terribly sorry to distress you," Chuck said. "Would you like for me to wait outside until you're finished tying those?"

"Don't be a nincompoop!" Maum snapped. "You'd

think my granddaughter would have checked before she brought a man in here, but I'm covered now."

Rizzie and Chuck smiled indulgently, but I knew how Maum felt. I used to think the same thing when I was a little girl and my brothers brought friends into the house unannounced.

"I really want to finish here," I said. "Unless you're just going to say 'hello,' why don't you wait in the dining room. Have something to eat and I'll be out before long."

"That works," Chuck said.

When Maum and I were done, I joined Chuck at the counter, where he was having a beer. "Let's move to a booth," he said.

Rizzie brought me a Diet Coke, and I leaned against the padded back of the seat.

"How'd you do at the show?" I asked.

"Didn't win first, but I placed. That ex-husband of yours is a jerk, did ya know that?"

"Why do you think I divorced him?"

"Why *did* you divorce him?"

"I don't want to talk about it. What made you know he's a jerk?"

"First, he got disqualified for having kit parts on a car he registered as completely authentic. Second, he told me to tell you that if your father needed an excellent cardiologist, you could have him called in. He'd even give you a discount!"

"What's wrong with that?"

"The dip stick should have come by here to check on your dad before he headed back to Columbia. After all, Uncle *is* his ex-father-in-law."

"Daddy never liked Donnie and Donnie didn't like him much either. So far as coming by to check on him, Daddy has an excellent doctor and is already home. He's doing fine, but he's going to have to make some healthy life changes."

"Do you think he's well enough for me to go by to see him?"

"Definitely. He'd love to see you. Actually, I'm off for the afternoon. Why don't you follow me over there?"

"I'd follow you to the ends of the earth."

"You are one sweet-talking man, even if you are my cousin."

"And you're one little Sweet Britches, even if you are my cousin."

# Chapter Twenty-Seven

"It's not gonna happen," Bill said emphatically, but his expression was miserable and apologetic. "I've talked myself blue in the face, and Molly insists there's no way to postpone the wedding."

"I'm stronger every day," Daddy said. "I told you not to even consider changing the date."

Chuck and I stood at the open door to my father's house and listened to Daddy and Bill. Daddy looked up from where he lay on the couch and waved us in.

"Just what I need—to see my favorite daughter and my favorite nephew." That wasn't saying a whole lot since Chuck and I are his only daughter and nephew. Now if he'd named a favorite son, it would have been a different matter.

"Want something to drink?" I asked them all—Daddy, Bill, and Chuck. They accepted. I handed Chuck and Bill beers from Daddy's drink fridge, which is against the back wall of the living room, and then asked, "Daddy, what are you drinking?"

"I'll take a beer, too," he said.

"No, he won't!" Bill jumped up and went to the refrigerator. "He's drinking decaffeinated tea. Anytime you're over here, his tea is in this pitcher, and this is his glass." Bill held up a squatty pitcher, poured a glassful from it and brought it over to Daddy. He handed me an ice cold Diet Coke.

Daddy grumbled but took a long swallow from his glass. "You might as well know the routine," Bill said. "Nothing fried, white meats with very rarely lean red meat, mainly fruits and vegetables, and don't add salt to anything—no alcohol or caffeine either."

"Might as well die," Daddy.

"Next time you might," Bill.

"Seems like you're feeling well enough to be ornery with your kids," Chuck said.

"Are you bed-ridden?" he added.

"No," Daddy said, "just supposed to take a rest after I eat. Then I have to take a walk, supposed to walk twice every day like running this farm isn't exercise enough."

"Well, if your rest time's up, let's take a walk," Chuck said.

They invited me to join them, but I declined. While Daddy made a stop in the restroom, I asked Bill, "What's this about delaying the wedding? Molly caught you up to something? Been hanging around cemeteries again?"

"No, I want to wait because of Pa. I'm afraid that with Frank over at yours and Jane's place and me moving in with Molly, he won't take care of himself. He'll go back to eating fried steak and gravy before I'm back from my honeymoon."

"I'll come by more often when you're not here. Didn't the doctor say it would be okay for him to stay alone?"

"Yes, but I'm . . ." Bill stopped talking when Daddy came back into the living room.

"Don't stop on my account," Daddy said. "I know you were talking about me."

"They were talking about how much we all love you," Chuck said. Bill's eyes widened. We all know we love each other, but Bill's never been demonstrative toward me or

Daddy.

When the men left, I went to Bill's computer in his room. I Googled the Buckley, New Jersey, Armored Car Robbery in 1980.

I printed out the news release for July 3, 1980:

Authorities in New Jersey have announced an arrest in one of the most unusual heists in U.S. history, but said that two fugitives remain on the loose.

The Ames County, N.J. sheriff's department alleges that Leon D. McDonald was involved in the June 30 robbery of an Armored car near Buckley which netted five million—more than half of the eight million the Northern Armored Car Services truck was carrying at the time.

Sheriff James Whitaker said law enforcement recovered less than $250,000 of the stolen money.

Leon McDonald has been charged with armed robbery, kidnapping, and aggravated assault and battery. He also faces a charge of conspiracy to commit burglary. He has refused to negotiate with law enforcement on any kind of deal to assist in locating the two men who were with him.

Additional suspects, John (Johnny) Johnson and Noah F. Gordon, have not been apprehended.

The Ames County sheriff is working on the investigation with the FBI and the New Jersey Law Enforcement Division.

That was interesting, but not nearly so much as the two photos. No doubt that the missing armored car robbers had recently been in Middleton's Mortuary. Passage of time and living wealthy had turned each of the men from rough-looking outlaws to elderly gentlemen, but I recognized Mr. Joyner and the Jaguar John Doe. Wonder how much of the loot they still had after so many years?

I called Wayne to tell him I wanted to show the article to him, but the dispatcher said the sheriff was out. He offered to ask Sheriff Harmon to call me as soon as the office heard from him.

Daddy lay down on the couch again when the men returned from their walk. Bill invited Chuck and me for dinner. After a few weak excuses that he needed to head on back to Florida, Daddy and Bill persuaded Chuck to stay.

"Won't be anything fit to eat," Daddy complained. "All I get around here now is chicken and fish. I keep telling Bill to fry us up some pork chops. After all, the TV says it's 'the other white meat.'"

Bill cooked while Daddy, Chuck, and I played cards. After an hour or so, I tried to call the sheriff again, but dispatch said they still hadn't heard anything from him.

Daddy had no cause to complain about the food. Bill served us grilled salmon, wild rice, and green beans for dinner with fresh fruit for dessert.

Chuck chowed down with doubles on just about everything, then excused himself to head home with promises to come back to see us "real soon." Bill hemmed and hawed around and finally asked me if I wanted to spend the night.

"No, I'll head on out of here if you two are ready for bed," I said. Then I looked carefully at my brother's face. He wasn't being *polite* inviting me to stay. He *wanted* me to spend the night.

"On second thought, I don't have anything pushing. I think I'll just hang around and watch television with Daddy," I said.

"In that case, I'm going to see Molly," Bill said. "See you in the morning."

"Have a good time," Daddy told him.

And I'll bet he did.

# Chapter Twenty-Eight

"Last time you had breakfast here, I cooked you grits and eggs and onion sausage and buttermilk biscuits with homemade preserves, so what is this nonsense you put in front of me?" Daddy sat at the kitchen table in his bathrobe and slippers. I'd gotten up early, showered, and dressed before I started cooking.

"Daddy, that's a perfectly good, healthy breakfast. Oatmeal and an egg white veggie omelet."

"If this is an omelet, where's the cheese? And ham or bacon?" Daddy took the fork and prodded at the food like a kid picking at a doodle bug.

"No wonder Bill doesn't want to leave you alone," I scolded. "You're behaving like a child. We just want to keep you alive. You're going to have to cooperate with us and eat what you're supposed to no matter who's with you. Isn't that what you'd tell me or one of The Boys if we'd had a heart attack?"

"I guess so if you put it that way," Daddy said, and began eating the omelet. He'd started on the oatmeal when the telephone rang. He grabbed it and barked, "Hello."

"Well, it's my danged phone. Who'd you expect to answer it?" Daddy continued and handed the receiver to me. "It's Bill and he needs to talk to *you*. Probably wants to know what you let me eat for breakfast. I don't see why he called *my* line to talk to *you*. He could have called your cell." He chuckled. "That is, if you remembered it."

"Hi Bill," I said, "He had oatmeal and an egg white omelet for breakfast. No, I didn't put bacon in it."

"That's good, but it's not what I called about," my brother said. "Turn your television to the local news."

"Hold on a minute," I answered.

"Just hang up and watch," Bill said.

"The press conference with Jade County Sheriff Wayne Harmon scheduled for yesterday's late night news and postponed until this morning's report is being cancelled." The news commentator cleared his throat, then continued, "Sheriff Harmon had called the conference to discuss the discovery that two men who died in Jade County have been identified as 'wanted' by the FBI for an armored car robbery in 1980. Sheriff Harmon's office reports that they have not been in contact with him since mid-day yesterday."

"What in Hades is that all about?" Daddy spluttered. "It's not like Wayne to schedule something and not show up."

The phone rang again. I answered this time. Bill said, "If you've already fed Pa, I'm going to ride over to Wayne's house and make sure he's not injured."

"Call me back and let us know what's going on," I said and disconnected the telephone.

"I'm going to get my shower and put on some regular clothes in case we have to go out," Daddy said. "Where's Mike?"

"He's either still in bed or didn't come home last night." I answered.

"No telling," Daddy said and got up.

"Do you need help?" I asked.

"I don't need *you* to shower me!" he snapped, got up, and headed for the bathroom. I cleaned up the dishes and sat down to watch for more news. The *Today* show was on and there was plenty of news, most of it depressing. None, however, was as disturbing to me as our local news had been.

"Get up, Calamine. I wanna go by Wayne's house and make sure he isn't there. Then we need to travel the routes he may have taken. He could have run off the road somewhere and the car's hidden in a gulley. It's not part of Wayne Harmon to neglect his duties like not showing up for a press con-ference, especially one he called himself." Daddy looked better than he had since his heart attack. He'd lost that apathetic expression he'd been wearing when the only thing he talked or thought about was what his next meal would be.

We were closing the front door behind us when Daddy said, "Calamine, get a Thermos out the cabinet and pour me up some of that decaffeinated tea to take with me. I got to get something else, too." I headed back to the kitchen.

I arrived at the Mustang in Daddy's driveway with a large Thermos of tea and two cans of cold Diet Coke. Daddy was sitting in the car with an old Colt .38 Police Special and a box of ammo on his lap. He said, "Unlock the glove compartment, so I can put these in it." I flipped it open for him, and we headed for Wayne Harmon's house.

My stomach turned a few flips and I felt like hurling when we arrived on the block where the sheriff lived. I could hardly see the front of his beige brick ranch-style home because cars were parked up and down the street as well as all over his lawn—police cars with blue lights flashing, unmarked law enforcement, news vans, and private ve-hicles like my brother Bill's bright purple truck. Fear filled me. They must have found Wayne. Was he hurt or was he dead?

As soon as I parked, Daddy got out and almost ran toward the house. One thing we knew for sure. Wayne hadn't run off the road. Both his sheriff's car and his personal Subaru were parked in the driveway. Bill saw Daddy, headed him off, and stopped him before I caught up with them.

"What's happening?" Daddy gasped, very out-of-breath. "How's Wayne?"

"We don't know. Wayne's not here. Apparently everyone had the same thought. You know—maybe our sheriff's 'fallen and can't get up.'" He chuckled and I popped him on the arm.

"It's not funny!" I snapped.

"Well, it's a relief that he's not in there injured or murdered."

"Murdered?"

"Any law man faces the risk that someone he's sent to jail will get out and come back to get even."

"We're not even going to think about that," Daddy said.

Some folks were bustling around while others stood still and ogled the front door. It opened and Fast Eddie Blake stepped out. He walked directly to us and asked, "How's Frank? I'm surprised Sheriff Harmon didn't put surveillance on him when the hospital dismissed him."

"He's improving," Bill said. "The main trouble he has now is some neurological problems. His hands and feet tingle like they're asleep. The doctors say that's good because it's more likely to improve than if they were completely numb."

"Good." Blake's face took on a smarmy look. "These people are wasting their time. The sheriff isn't here even though both of his cars are. He's been going out with that

FBI woman. I tried to tell them he probably thinks he's that governor. You know the one who just took off a week or so for some South American delight without telling anyone where he was going."

"That's not something Wayne would do," Daddy said.

"There's nothing we can do here," Bill interrupted. He obviously didn't want to let Daddy get started with the smart-alecky deputy. He turned toward me. "I'll take Pa back to our house and you might want to go home and check on Jane. I talked to Frank a while ago, and he said she's sick as a dog."

Daddy argued that there ought to be something else we could do, but when he couldn't name a suggestion, he agreed to go home with Bill.

I was on the way to Jane's and my apartment when I remembered Daddy had left the gun in the car. I thought I was within the law to have it locked in the glove compartment, but after all that hullabaloo when Jane and I went to pick up the basket casket, I figured I'd take it back to Daddy as soon as possible.

# Chapter Twenty-Nine

The sound of a woman throwing up is unpleasant at best. I know this for a fact since I barf anytime I'm frightened. Jane added to the retching sound by moaning and groaning both before and after each episode. She also screamed, "Get out of here. Don't look at me like this!" every time Frankie opened the bathroom door. The scene was so bad that Big Boy hid behind the couch.

"But, honey, I just want to wipe your face with this wet cloth," Frankie said and waved a dripping wash cloth in the air. He turned and saw me. "Callie's here," he said. "Can she come in and help you?"

"I don't need any help. I want to be left alone until this is over." She kicked at the door and Frankie pulled it closed.

"How long has she been like this?" I asked, crowding behind him.

"Since she woke up. Should I take her to the ER?" My brother looked terrified.

"No, it's probably a virus. If it doesn't end soon, we can call the doctor for something to stop it."

"I keep thinking maybe she's been exposed to whatever poisoned me. My first sign I was sick was nausea, violent nausea."

"I hadn't thought of that. Maybe we should call someone."

"Who? Does she have a regular doctor?"

"I don't think so. I'll call Dr. Donald."

"I'll make some coffee."

Miracles never cease. Donald wasn't on duty, but when I called his private cell phone, he answered immediately. I explained what was happening, and he said, "So long as you promise to never, ever tell anyone I did this, I'll run by, but don't describe it as a house call. Doctors don't make those anymore." He paused. "Where does Jane live?"

"In the other side of the duplex I lived in when you came over here."

"I'm not too far away. Be there soon, and I'll bring something to help the nausea."

I sat on the couch sipping my java until Jane began yelling that the smell of the coffee was making her feel worse. Frankie poured his cup down the sink. I really wanted that coffee, so I took Big Boy to the front porch with me, sat on the step, and drank my brew while I waited for Donald.

The first time I ever saw Dr. Donald Walters, even before we dated, was in the hospital emergency room when I had a concussion. I remember thinking how fine he looked. Later, after I learned how many women he dated, I decided he was too good looking for me. I don't want a man who's chased by every female he meets and generally lets each one catch him.

Today, Donald looked great. I would have known he was off even if he hadn't told me. He had on jeans and a tan T-shirt. Muscles rippled, and his blue eyes sparkled. I would have known he was a doctor, too. He was carrying a little black bag like they do on television.

Frankie explained the situation to Donald. "She's been doing this off and on for several weeks." He didn't have to explain what "this" was. We could hear Jane heaving even though the bathroom door was closed. "I'm afraid that she's been exposed to whatever put me in the hospital."

"That's not likely," the doctor answered. "Unless she were being given minute amounts of poison consistently, she'd either get sick and get over it or get sick and continue to get worse and worse." He knocked lightly on the bathroom door and called, "Jane, Jane. This is Donald Walters, the doctor. May I come in and see if I can help you?"

"No, I'm beginning to feel better. It'll go away and then I'll come out. Ask Frankie to hand me the wet cloth he had." Frankie opened the door a few inches and passed the fabric through to her.

"Is that coffee I smell?" Donald asked.

"We had some, but I dumped it because Jane said it was making her sicker," Frankie said.

"That's interesting," Donald said.

The three of us sat on the couch and watched television as the sounds of Jane's nausea subsided. When the local news came on, we all sat up a little straighter as though that would make us hear better. The beginning of the broadcast showed the earlier scene at Sheriff Harmon's house. I even saw Bill's purple truck. The commentator reported that the sheriff was missing and there was no sign of him in his home though both of his vehicles were there.

Jane emerged from the bathroom just as an interview with one of the long-time deputies assured the public that everything possible was being done to locate Sheriff Harmon. She looked washed-out and pale, but she smiled.

"Do you think Sheriff Harmon has run off with some woman?" she asked.

"No!" Frankie and I blurted together.

"Wayne would run off with a woman if he had time

off," Frankie said, "or if he notified his people where he would be, but no way would he just abandon his responsibilities. Something's wrong, but it's hard to figure out what since both cars are at his house according to the news."

"Both cars *are* there," I said. "Daddy and I went over there this morning."

"Was that jerk, Eddie, there?" asked Frankie.

"Yes," I said, "and as a matter of fact, he asked about you. You know he's who arrested Mike for the open container for having the keg in the truck, don't you?"

Frankie said, "Yes," but Donald asked what we were talking about.

He chuckled after Frankie explained it, then turned to Jane. "Young lady, I think you need something in your stomach."

"Oh, no," Jane moaned. "I don't want anything to eat."

Donald turned to me. "Get her some saltines and gingerale. She'll be sick again unless she gets something down."

I went to the kitchen area and returned with a saucer of saltines and a juice glass of Seven Up since we didn't have any gingerale.

"Take the liquid in small sips and the crackers in tiny bites," Donald said. He pulled a pen and one of his cards from his pocket. He wrote a name on the back of the card and handed it to Jane. "Later today," he said, "have Callie call and make you an appointment with this doctor. You need a complete check-up."

He rose and started toward the door. I followed him, and Big Boy followed me.

At the door, Donald said, "That puppy of yours has really grown."

"Yes, he has," I agreed and noticed he was looking at

my chest. I wished I had on one of my inflatable bras.

He grinned and I knew he was remembering the same time I was when we were both feeling romantic, but my puppy had brought everything to a screeching halt. That was before I learned Donald's a playboy.

"Do I owe you anything?" I asked, meaning was there a charge for his coming to check on Jane though he hadn't actually done anything for her.

"Well, I think I do have a rain check from you," he said, "but we won't worry about that with Jane and your brother here."

I waved goodbye and, for some reason, went to my bedroom and changed bras. Just to be complete, I put on a pair of my fanny panties, too. They're made to provide a lift. I wondered why "panties," which is, or are, one garment are plural and come in "pairs," while "bra" is singular and seems more suited to being called a "pair."

My analysis came to an end when Frankie yelled, "Come here, Callie. There's a local newsflash."

The same reporter's face showed on the screen. "The FBI has been called into the investigation of the disappearance of Jade County Sheriff Wayne Harmon. Sheriff Harmon has been working with FBI Special Agent Georgette Randolph on the 1980 armored car robbery in Buckley, New Jersey. When attempts were made to contact Agent Randolph for any clues to Harmon's whereabouts, Agent Randolph was found to be missing also. Stay tuned for more on our noon local news report."

Frankie pounded his fist on the couch. "I don't believe it!" he shouted. "Wayne would not just take off with some woman while on a case. He wouldn't call a press conference and not show up. Something's mighty wrong here."

Jane's face paled again. "What's the matter?" I asked. "Do you know something about the sheriff?"

"No," she wailed and dashed back to the restroom. When she came out, she grinned, "I don't know why, but those saltines are helping. I didn't even throw up this time."

"Good," I said. "I think I'm going over to Daddy's and make sure he and Bill know about this."

"Give me the card Dr. Walters gave you," Frankie said to Jane, "and I'll call for an appointment."

"I feel better now," Jane said.

"The doctor said a full checkup," Frankie insisted. Jane handed him the card, and Frankie was dialing the telephone when I left.

# Chapter Thirty

"Put the gun back in the safe," I told myself when I headed away from St. Mary toward Daddy's house. I grew up around rifles, shotguns, and pistols since not only do Daddy and The Boys hunt, they tend to collect any firearm someone is broke enough to sell at a huge discount. I don't like hunting, but I'm pretty good at target practice.

My next thoughts were about Wayne Harmon. Where could he be? *Why* would he just disappear and was that Georgette woman with him?

*Dalmation!* All of a sudden, my mind jumped from guns and missing sheriffs to what I'd heard Bill tell Daddy. "Molly won't postpone the wedding." Next he'd be saying, "And Molly's mad at all of us because Callie won't go get her dress fitted."

I looked carefully in all directions, then made a U-turn and headed back into St. Mary and the bridal shop. I heard the siren before I saw the blue light, but I knew in my heart that the blare was for me. I pulled off the road and parked on the shoulder. When I rolled down the window, I heard those words, "License and registration, please."

"Hello, Deputy Blake," I said as I handed him the papers.

"Don't try to smooth talk me," he said, "I'm writing

you a ticket for that U-turn."

*One hundred and one Dalmations!* I thought. *Being nice to him is a waste of time, but maybe he'll listen to reason.* Of course, I was thinking of *my* kind of reason, not *his*!

"There's no one around," I began.

"*I'm* around," he said.

I didn't mean to, I promise I didn't mean to, but I sassed him. "Then write the ticket and let me go. I'm in a hurry."

"I could take you in for assaulting an officer of the law with that nasty attitude," he said.

"I don't think that's a real charge. Besides, wouldn't it make more sense for you to be trying to locate your missing boss?" I asked as he handed me the pale blue paper and explained that I could pay the fine or show up in court at the time and date written on the ticket.

"Yes, and that's why I'm not going to bother, but you need an attitude check, young lady!"


By the time I reached the dress store, I'd calmed down. The clerk was very accommodating and led me to the main dressing room—the big one where brides try on gowns. The peach-pumpkin-orange dress didn't look as bad on me as I'd expected. Of course, that could have been because of the underwear I had on. My sister-in-law Miriam had been right. My hair looked great with it. I'd been considering changing my hair color before the wedding, but the auburn was perfect.

"Lovely, just lovely," the sales lady said. "That dress could have been made for you."

The gowns had been special ordered. I thought that meant my dress *was* made for me. When I'd changed back into my jeans, she said the words I'd been expecting.

"We have your deposit, but it's customary to finish

paying in full when the dress is fitted."

Yep, I knew that was coming. I pulled my wallet from my purse, but my Visa card wasn't in it. I have this bad habit of dropping cards into my handbag instead of putting them back where they belong after I use them. I sat down and dumped my pocket book onto the chair beside me. I began picking through the receipts, makeup, and other junk in there, but I couldn't find the credit card. I pulled out a folded newspaper. It was the 1980 newspaper backing my ex had used for his sign at the car show. I'd totally forgotten it was still in my purse. When I shook the paper, my Visa fell onto the floor. I leaned over, picked up the card, and dropped the newspaper. It lay upside down on the mauve carpet, and a familiar face stared up at me.

I didn't feel like hurling. I wasn't scared. I was shocked.

When I handed the credit card to the lady, she began explaining the charges to me and the discount she was giving to Molly's attendants because she'd once bought a poodle from Molly. I cut her off rudely. "I'm in a hurry. Just let me sign the charge."

In the car, I couldn't decide where to go. If Sheriff Harmon weren't missing, I would have called him immediately to tell him what I'd discovered. At least I had my cell phone with me, fully charged, too. I knew of no way to reach the sheriff. The whole point was to find him. I tried to think of places he could be. Suddenly I remembered his talking about his fishing cabin on the lake. I headed that way.

# Chapter Thirty-One

What was the quickest way to the cabin? I'd been there lots of times with my brothers. Lots of good times cleaning and frying fish Wayne and The Boys had just caught while I'd sunned myself and read a book. Now I was flying down the road toward the lake, ignoring fear that Fast Eddie Blake would catch me for speeding. Thoughts all a-jumble. Scared of Blake, yet almost hoping he would stop me before I got to the cabin. Praying that I'd find Wayne there alive.

As I turned off the paved highway onto the rutted dirt road to the cabin, I leaned across the seat and took out Daddy's Colt .38. Talking on cell phones while driving is hazardous. Try loading a gun while driving. I didn't think I should wait until I'd stopped to take care of it.

The first thing I saw in the driveway was a tan Jade County Sheriff's Deputy car. Maybe Wayne's vehicle needed repairs and he'd taken a different unit to come up here to think about the poisonings. Perhaps he *was* with Special Agent Randolph. If they'd come up here for some privacy, I was about to shatter it. Then again, if he'd borrowed another Jade County vehicle, he would have checked it out. The department would know about it, and so would the news commentators.

I parked the Mustang as quietly as possible, bypassed the partially open front door, and crept to the uncurtained window at the side of the building. I knew from the past that the cabin was a large open room with the front door in one corner, kitchen area in another, bed in the third, and door to the bathroom on the remaining wall. I'm no Stephanie Plum! She would have hesitated to carry her usually unloaded gun, having left it in her cookie jar or some other ridiculous place. My arms were stretched out in front of me with both hands clutching the ready-to-fire weapon in a SWAT team pose.

Frozen at the window, I saw and heard a scene that was real but hard to believe. The FBI agent lay across the bed, blindfolded, gagged, and handcuffed to the bedpost. Her face was expressionless, and she wasn't moving.

Wayne sat in a captain's chair with his left hand and both feet cuffed to the chair. His right arm stretched out across the old wooden table where I'd eaten so many fried fish. A piece of rope tied his hand to the table top. His face twisted with anguish.

"Tell me where the money is or I'll break another finger," the man standing over Harmon said. I saw the hammer he held at the same time he crashed it down on the sheriff's bound hand. I'll never forget Wayne's shriek.

"I don't know where the money is," Wayne moaned after he stopped screaming.

"You know where it is. That's the reason you called the press conference, but that money is mine. I'm entitled to it. I spent years tracking down Johnson and Gordon.

"My mistake was sending those prints to AFIS. I was trying to impress you with my efficiency, but I had no idea they'd come from one of my victims and would lead to reopening the investigation. Those men let my father take the whole rap. They were living like rich men while he was beaten and stabbed to death in prison." He spat on the floor. "Now tell me how to find the loot while you still have one unbroken finger."

"I swear we don't know where the money is." Wayne's voice was barely a whisper. "The press conference was for me to show pictures of Johnny Johnson and Noah Gordon and ask for public assistance from anyone who's seen or known them. Someone must have had contact with them during the past thirty years." He stopped and turned his head toward the bed. "What have you done to her? Did you give her poison?"

"No poison, just something to make her sleep while I get answers from you. Don't worry about your lady friend. I know what I'm doing. The resume I gave you substituted 'Criminal Justice' for my Master's degree in Chemistry. You should make it a point to check letters of recommendation from previous employers. I forged mine." The man laughed. "I'll give you both some of what Johnny Johnson got plus an even bigger poisonous snake if you don't tell me where the money is." He nodded toward the woman on the bed. "I'm sure you've thought about sleeping with her. When I finish, you two can sleep together eternally if you don't cooperate with me."

I gasped.

"What's that?" The man pounded the hammer on the table again, and Wayne screeched in agony. I took off running before the attacker got to the window. I didn't sprint toward my car or into the woods. I darted directly to the front door and jumped inside with the .38 pointed straight at Fast Eddie Blake's face, the same face that had stared up at me from the 1980 newspaper.

"I'm not scared of you," he said, but he stopped in his tracks.

"If he makes one move toward you, shoot him," Harmon said.

"No skirt is going to shoot me," Blake said, "especially some little hick piece like you."

He raised the hammer, but I think that was meant to

distract me because he also reached for the Glock .40 in his holster.

I shot him.

# Chapter Thirty-Two

"Here Comes the Bride" had played. I'd actually stood at the front of the church beside a poodle dyed to match the pumpkin-colored dress I wore. When the minister asked for the rings, I'd obediently untied them from the bow in the dog's topnotch and handed those circular golden symbols of fidelity to the pastor. Bill and Molly had "I do-ed" themselves into positions that were supposed to last 'til death did them part, and the best time of that fancy wedding had arrived—the reception!

Sheriff Harmon stood beside me. I appreciated his attention because my date had been called away right before the wedding began. Wayne's right arm was in a sling with all fingers splinted. He'd bragged to everyone how smart I was to come to the fishing cabin for him and how brave I was to shoot the deputy.

I insisted that going to the fishing cabin was a stroke of lucky first guess inspired by hearing him and Blake talk about fishing. Knowing who the villain was had been fate—destined by my messy purse. I'd actually cleaned the handbag out since that horrible day at the cabin. Fast Eddie Blake was the spittin' image of his father Leon McDonald, the third member of the group of robbers in Buckley, New Jersey, in 1980—the face that had stared up at me from that old newspaper. Of course, Fast Eddie Blake was actually Edward McDonald.

Leon McDonald's son had sought out the men who'd lived lives of leisure after his father died penniless in prison. The men had been easier to find than the money, which Harmon insisted still hadn't been located.

"I didn't mean to kill him," I said to Sheriff Harmon for the umpteenth time. "I only wanted to stop him."

"Quit sweating what happened," the sheriff answered.

"I don't sweat," I said. "Daddy says horses sweat, men perspire, and ladies glisten."

Wayne laughed. He'd heard that line before.

"You may not like it, Callie," he said, "but sometimes the only way to stop a murderer is to kill him. Some folks deserve to die, and don't forget you saved my life as well as your own and Georgette's. Eddie would have killed all of us."

Levi joined the sheriff and me. Loose Lucy was at his side.

"Callie," she burbled. "I requested a song for you."

The band's front man announced, "Everyone, listen up now. We've got a special song dedicated to Miss Callie Parrish."

They broke into "I Shot the Sheriff" with a slight change in lyrics. They sang, "I did not shoot the sheriff but I shot the deputy down." The crowd burst into shouts and applause. Levi and Lucy headed for the punch bowl.

I blushed and tried to continue my conversation with the sheriff. "What I don't understand is why Blake poisoned my brother. He was out for revenge and money with Johnson and Gordon, but why Frankie?"

Wayne Harmon leaned in close to my ear. "Blake didn't poison Frankie. Jane did!"

"No way!" I blurted.

"By accident. Frank knows it, but there's no point in making an issue of it. When we confiscated poisonous items from the house, a deputy removed a can of lemon-scented roach spray from the cabinet. One of the things Jane left for Frank's lunch was his favorite lemon bars. The baking dish they were cooked in was in the sink. It tested positive for the roach spray poison, which normally is fatal to roaches but doesn't harm humans—unless the person ingests a sizeable amount. Jane sprayed the dish with what she thought was Pam. She didn't catch the difference in the scent because the batter smelled like lemons. I've had a long talk with Frank about not moving things if one lives with a visually handicapped person."

"I learned that the first time I lived with Jane," I said, "but the results were a nasty dinner, not a poisoning."

"Frank asked me not to say anything to her because he was the one who last used the bug spray and he was the one who made a pig of himself and ate an entire dish of lemon bars, consuming a lot of the spray. He swears they didn't taste bad."

"Thank you for not telling Jane," I said.

"This thing hurts." Wayne pointed his left hand to his right. "I'm heading home." He looked around. "I see Otis and Odell here. Who's minding the mortuary? Denise or Darlene?"

"Darlene left yesterday. Just like Odell said, those two can only put up with so much of each other. Denise is manning my desk, and she'll even stay after dark because Odell discovered a cat in the attic with three baby kittens. That's what Denise heard and thought were ghost sounds."

"How about Big Boy? Has he recovered from the neutering?"

I blushed again. "I haven't had time to take him. I missed his appointment and have to reschedule."

Wayne looked across the room and said, "I see your date has arrived."

Dr. Donald Walters walked toward us. Knowing I

wasn't dating anyone special and that bridesmaids hate to be without an escort, he'd invited me to come with him. Problem was that he'd been called in on an emergency right after we arrived at the church. He approached Wayne and me with a sheepish, apologetic look.

"Sorry," he said. "I had no idea it would take so long. Thanks for taking care of my date, Sheriff Harmon."

"No problem, but I'm glad you're here. This hand is giving me fits. I'm going home, take a pain pill, and lie down."

"That's the thing to do. The body needs rest to heal."

Donald and I danced a few times. He asked, "How's Jane?"

"She's fine. She and Frank are leaving from here to go to the mountains."

"Has she been to the doctor yet?"

"That's next week."

"You know what's wrong with her, don't you?" Donald asked when we stopped dancing and went for punch.

"Is she pregnant?" I questioned as Donald handed me a punch cup.

"That's for the doctor to tell her," he said.

"You're a doctor." I confess I cut him a flirtatious look.

"I'm not *her* doctor, but I want to be *your* doctor."

"You are. Every time anyone in my family is hurt or sick, you're there. You've been my doctor when I was hospitalized with concussions, too."

"That's not what I mean, and you know it."

"I haven't heard any recent rumors that you're dating every female that goes through the hospital," I said.

"I'm not. I'm looking for one woman and I want to be a one-woman man." He surprised me so much that my cup of orange punch spilled all over my dress. Donald tried to wipe it off with napkins, and it was hard to ignore his touch.

"I want to go home," I said.

"You don't want to try to catch the bride's bouquet?" he asked.

"Not really. I'd rather go to the apartment and change."

The ride in the doctor's new Porsche was comfortable except for the wet dress. When we arrived, Big Boy met us at the door with his leash in his mouth. Donald took him for a walk while I changed. I'd showered and slipped into shorts and a T-shirt when they came back into the apartment. Big Boy rushed to me in my room. Donald followed him.

"So I finally get to see your bedroom," he said.

I didn't say anything. He took me in his arms, hugged me, and kissed me. The kiss started out very tender, but it didn't take long to turn hot. I kissed back.

"Are you thinking what I'm thinking?" he asked softly.

I didn't say a word, led Big Boy into the living room, and returned to my bedroom.

I closed the door.

## The End

# About the Author

**Fran Rizer** is the author of the Callie Parrish Mysteries. She lives in South Carolina. Readers may learn more about her, check out recipes for some of the foods mentioned in the books, and correspond with her on the website.

www.franrizer.com

CPSIA information can be obtained at www.ICGtesting.com
Printed in the USA
BVOW031713031212

307147BV00001B/115/P